'If you fail to live up to her expectations you will regret it.'

For several moments Anna remained too shocked by her own thought processes to respond.

'Is that a threat, Mr Urquart?' she finally asked quietly.

His dark eyebrows rose upwards. 'It is a fact, Miss Henderson,' he responded, without missing a beat.

Anna's chin lifted and her blue eyes narrowed at the corners, darkening with purpose as she met his stare head-on. Excitement was not a sane response to the warning, yet it was there in the shiver that slid like a silken finger down her spine.

Kim Lawrence comes from English/Irish stock. Though lacking much authentic Welsh blood, she was born and brought up in North Wales. She returned there when she married, and her sons were both born on Anglesey, an island off the coast. Though not isolated, Anglesey is a little off the beaten track, but lively Dublin, which Kim loves, is only a short ferry-ride away.

Today they live on the farm her husband was brought up on. Welsh is the first language of many people in this area and Kim's husband and sons are all bilingual—she is having a lot of fun, not to mention a few headaches, trying to learn the language!

When she had small children, the unsocial hours of nursing didn't look attractive—so, encouraged by a husband who thinks she can do anything she sets her mind to, Kim tried her hand at writing. Always a keen Harlequin Mills & Boon reader, it seemed natural for her to write a romance novel—now she can't imagine doing anything else.

She is a keen gardener and cook and enjoys running— often on the beach, as the sea is never very far away. She is usually accompanied by her Jack Russell, Sprout—don't ask...it's long story!

Recent titles by the same author:

MAID FOR MONTERO *(At His Service)*
THE PETRELLI HEIR
SANTIAGO'S COMMAND
GIANNI'S PRIDE

CAPTIVATED BY HER INNOCENCE

BY
KIM LAWRENCE

First published in Great Britain 2013
by Mills & Boon, an imprint of Harlequin (UK) Limited.
Harlequin (UK) Limited, Eton House, 18-24 Paradise Road,
Richmond, Surrey TW9 1SR

© Kim Lawrence 2013

ISBN: 978 0 263 23536 4

Harlequin (UK) policy is to use papers that are natural, renewable and recyclable products and made from wood grown in sustainable forests. The logging and manufacturing process conform to the legal environmental regulations of the country of origin.

Printed and bound in Great Britain
by CPI Antony Rowe, Chippenham, Wiltshire

CAPTIVATED BY HER INNOCENCE

CHAPTER ONE

IF PRACTICE DID, as they claimed, make perfect, then Anna's smile would be delivering just the right mixture of cool, collected confidence and deference. Beneath her neatly buttoned pink tweed jacket, however, her heart was thudding so hard that she had an image of it battering its way through her ribcage as she reeled off her opinion of the recent changes in the primary school curriculum.

Her heart stayed in place and, speaking with the appropriate level of confidence, she held her audience's attention—or behind their intent looks were they actually planning their evening meals?

Anna lifted her chin and pushed away the doubts. She told herself to relax, and if she messed up? Well, it was only a job. Only a job? Who was she kidding?

The philosophical attitude might fool the rest of the world but this was not just any job for Anna—a fact she had realised when her two interview dates had clashed. The choice seemed simple, between a highly regarded local school within walking distance of her flat, where it had been hinted, strictly off the record, that she was a very strong candidate, or the post at a remote school on the north-west coast of Scotland—a job she wouldn't have even applied for had she not seen that article in the dentist's waiting room.

Clearly a no-brainer, and yet here she was desiring this job more than she had wanted anything in a long time.

'Of course, we all want young people to turn into rounded individuals but discipline is important, don't you think, Miss Henderson?'

Anna tipped her head and nodded gravely. 'Of course.' She focused on the thin woman at the far end of the line-up who had posed the question before including the rest of the panel. 'But I think in an atmosphere where every child feels valued and is encouraged to reach their potential, discipline is rarely a problem. At least that has been my experience in the classroom.'

The balding man sitting to her right glanced down at the paper in front of him.

'And this experience has been almost exclusively in city schools?' A significant glance and wry smile was shared with his panel members. 'A crofting community like this one is not exactly what you have been used to, is it?'

Anna, who had been anticipating this question, relaxed and nodded. Her friends and family had already voiced the same opinion, only not so tactfully, implying that she'd lose the will to live within a month in this cultural desert! Ironically the only people who hadn't offered a negative opinion had been the ones who probably hated the idea more than anyone else.

If Aunt Jane and Uncle George, whose only daughter

had recently made her home in Canada, had thrown up their hands in horror at the prospect of the niece they had always treated like a second daughter leaving too, it would have been understandable but, no, the couple had remained their normal, quietly supportive selves.

'True but...'

A page was turned and bushy brows lifted. 'It says here you have a good working knowledge of Gaelic?'

'I'm rusty, but until I was eight I lived on Harris. My dad was a vet. I only moved to London after my parents' death.' Anna had no memory of the horrific accident that she had escaped totally unscathed. People had called it a miracle but Anna thought miracles were kinder. 'So working and living in the Highlands would be return-ing to my roots, something I have always wanted to do.'

This conviction that her life, if not her frozen heart, belonged in the Highlands had made her ignore advice and push ahead with her application for the post of head teacher at this tiny primary school in an isolated but beautiful part of the Scottish north-west coast.

This was not a knee-jerk reaction to her ex, Mark, or the near-miss wedding and she was most definitely not running away!

Teeth gritted, she pushed away the thought and lifted her chin. Mark, who she had never persuaded to take a holiday anywhere without sun and sand let alone north of the border, would have been bewildered by her choice but his bewilderment was no longer a factor. She was a free agent and she wished him and his underwear model all the happiness they both richly deserved, and if that involved the stick thin blonde gaining a hundred pounds all the better! Anna might not be heartbroken or devastated—she had seen devastated and had taken active steps to avoid it—but she was human.

She'd show the doubters that she could do it, but she had to get the job first. Shaking off her doubts, she focused on staying positive, desperately hoping it was enough to convince the panel to give her a chance.

So far, so good. Was this sliver of optimism inviting fate to cut her down to size? Anna blinked away the thought and focused on the question being asked, determined not to blow it now when it was going so well. She was not, as she had half expected, simply there to make up the numbers. Instead it was wide open: she really had a shot here.

It was going well.

Very well, she corrected mentally as the chairman of the panel leaned back in his seat and looked at her over his half-rimmed spectacles and produced his first smile.

'Well, Miss Henderson, thank you very much for coming today. Is there anything you'd like to ask us?'

Anna, who had compiled a list of intelligent and practical questions for this moment, found herself shaking her head.

'Then if you'd like to wait in the staff room we won't keep you in suspense long, but I think I can speak for us all when I say that you have impressed—'

Anna, who had got to her feet and smoothed down her skirt, stifled a frustrated sigh as after a short knock the door to her left opened, causing the interviewer to leave this promising sentence incomplete. A moment later it was not the cold air from the draughty corridor that made her gasp but the person who entered the room.

He had to be used to gasps, looking as he did. He was something special.

Early thirties? Several inches over six feet, lean, broad shoulders, endless long legs, athletically muscular and absolutely stunningly gorgeous! Possessing a wide, sensually moulded mouth, dark, thickly lashed heavily lidded eyes, and the sort of strong, chiselled features that a Greek statue would have envied, the new arrival ticked every box on Anna's personal list of attributes required of dark brooding hero, from the top of his dark, tousled, damp head to his mud splashed shoes.

Past the static buzz in her head, Anna registered the vibrant timbre of his deep voice but not what he said to the members of the panel—not the words maybe, but she did get the aura of raw masculinity he projected. It would have been hard not to!

Along with sex, he literally exuded authority from every perfect pore. Was it possible that this identikit Hollywood action-hero figure was the missing interview panel member whose absence had been apologised for?

Anna hadn't given the no-show another thought, but if this was him she could see that his tardiness had been a stroke of luck for her, given the fact she was struggling and failing to hold his gaze without falling victim to a deep, very un-head-teacher-like blush, and shamefully the heat was not confined to her previously pale cheeks! The chances that she would have been able to manage an entire interview without doing something mortifying were slim. It was all very disturbing, possibly due to the accumulated stress of an interview on top of the long journey north. Whatever its cause, she had never in her life experienced a physical reaction like this to a man before—even her scalp was tingling.

Mortified and bemused by her reaction, she clasped her clammy hands together in a grip that turned her knuckles white as she struggled to control this over-the-top reaction. Then he was looking away, thank goodness. Anna shook her head to clear the shivering a moment later, a response to the touch of the dark eyes that brushed her face again. She had never stepped off a high cliff into velvety pitch darkness but she was pretty sure that if she did it would feel this way!

The intense, narrow-eyed stare was not intended to make the recipient feel warm and fluffy, that was for sure. For a moment she thought she had glimpsed a flicker of recognition in those steel-grey depths, but then it was gone and she was valiantly struggling to re-gain some of her shattered composure when the chair-man of the interview panel, a local councillor, made the necessary introductions.

'Cesare, this is Miss Henderson, our last, though in no way least, candidate.'

The smile sent Anna's way was warm with approval.

'There are tea and biscuits in the office. Mrs Sinclair will look after you.' The chairman stepped to one side to allow Anna access to the door and turned his head to address his next comment to the tall man with the Italian-sounding name and the glowing olive-toned complexion. 'Miss Henderson was just leaving us for a moment while we—'

The speculation buzzing in Anna's head was louder than the flock of seagulls outside.

Cesare—the name was as un-British as his looks if you discounted the spookily pale silver-grey eyes. So what was his story?

The answer was not long coming, or at least part of it.

'Miss Henderson, this is Cesare Urquart. He is the reason the school enjoys the connections with local businesses you were so complimentary about.'

Anna was so flustered she barely recalled her name, let alone the comment she had made earlier.

'Mr Urquart.' Relieved she sounded relatively sane despite her temporary but dramatic hormone imbalance, Anna tipped her head back and in the process found herself on the receiving end of a penetrating and distinctly chilly stare.

'Anna was also very impressed by our green credentials.' The older man appeared oblivious to the weird undercurrents—did that mean it was all in her head?

Her hand on the door handle, she paused as he added, 'It is thanks to Cesare's generosity and foresight that the school not only produces enough electricity for itself but sells it back to the grid. There was talk at one point of the school closing like so many other small schools before Cesare took a personal interest.'

There was a pause, and Anna knew a response was expected. So she nodded and made an admiring noise in the back of her throat, but would it kill the man to smile?

'I have a personal interest.'

The woman on the panel spoke up. 'And how is little Jasmine? We have all missed her, Killaran.'

'Bored.'

So rich and influential Mr Urquart—or Killaran?— appeared to be a parent. Presumably with the child came a wife and mother who was his glamorous female equivalent? Rich incomers who had bought their way into the hearts of the locals? Her cynicism allowed room for the possibility their motives might be totally altruistic. Either way she knew there were many small schools under threat of closure who would have envied the village their rich benefactor. It was just sad that they needed one.

'Miss Henderson.' Cesare Urquart took a step her way and her grip on the door handle tightened. She was forced to tilt her head back to meet his eyes and she shifted her weight from one foot to the other feeling more like an errant schoolgirl than a prospective headmistress. 'I must apologise for my late arrival.'

He didn't sound sorry, and the smile that he gave did not reach his spectacular eyes. Anna was receiving the strong unspoken message that this disturbingly handsome man did not like her. Fair enough, she didn't particularly like him. She returned his smile with one of equal insincerity. She might not have been as good an actor as he was because she saw a flash in his eyes before she brought her lashes down in a protective shield.

'You have no objection if I ask you a little about yourself?' he asked. Like *wrecked any marriages recently*?

Of course he knew the answer. Women like her rarely

changed; they sailed through life leaving a trail of destruction in their selfish wake.

'Of course not,' Anna lied as Cesare Urquart shrugged off the dark cashmere overcoat he wore to reveal an elegant grey suit and a body that appeared to consist of solid muscle. She was shocked to feel desire clutch low in her belly and averted her shamed stare, focusing hard on her steepled fingers pressed together until her knuckles went white.

She had to get a grip—the atmosphere had definitely changed.

Cesare had walked into the room, seen a beautiful woman and felt a visceral stab of attraction that hadn't diminished even after he had recognised her and experienced a deluge of outraged anger. Anger so extreme that he had literally been a reckless breath away from confronting her right there, outing her in front of the panel.

Fortunately the shock had flattened out, though not the testosterone-fuelled heat in his belly. Hormones were indiscriminate things; however, he was not. He had not allowed his hormones to rule him since he was a schoolboy.

He firmly believed a man could not be in control of any situation unless he was in control of himself. Cesare liked to be in control.

Like any other situation, this one needed a cool, analytical approach. When he applied this rule two things were clear to him: she was the last woman on the planet equipped with the moral authority to be a head teacher, and she had won over the interview panel.

And to be fair, had he been meeting her for the first

time, even with his razor-sharp instincts for reading people, he might not have guessed that a first-class immoral bitch hid behind the angelic face. Even given his insider knowledge it was a struggle to reconcile what he knew her to be capable of with the guileless, quite disturbingly direct bright blue stare.

He did not allow the seeds of doubt to take hold; neither did he doubt his ability to convince the other panel members, help them see beyond the sexy librarian suit and the smile, that she was the wrong person for the job. He would be totally impartial while he gave her the chance to prove it for him.

As he took his seat behind the long table his attention was drawn to the gleaming top of her head. On the occasion when he had last seen her his attention had been captured, not by this woman's colouring, but what she had been doing, namely publicly devouring the face of his married best friend!

Even with his attention on other things, under the subdued lights of the restaurant her hair, cut into a sleek jaw-length style, had been definably auburn. But under the harsh, unforgiving electric light of this room, grown long enough now to twist into a neat knot that revealed the long, smooth curve of her throat, it shone as bright as flame, rich, dramatic, glossy copper interwoven with threads of bright gold.

Paul always had had a thing for redheads—some had even been natural—but he had married a blonde and despite this woman's attempts to wreck that marriage he still was.

Cesare continued to study the face of the woman who

had almost cost his friend his marriage and felt desire as indiscriminate as it was strong twist in his belly.

He could recognise his response, see it for what it was: a primal male reaction to a beautiful woman. Paul hadn't, but then his friend always had been a hopeless romantic, frequently making the classic mistake of confusing sex with love.

The night in question Paul had followed him out of the restaurant, catching him up as he was about to get in his car. 'It isn't what you think.'

Cesare had not responded to his friend's breathless opening statement. It was not his place to give the approval Paul clearly sought, though why a grown man would need it mystified Cesare.

'You won't say anything to Clare? All right, sorry, sorry, I know you wouldn't.'

Slamming the door of his car, Cesare had turned back to his friend... How could an intelligent man be so stupid? 'Someone will tell her, though—you must see that. You were hardly being discreet.'

'I know, I know, but it's Rosie's birthday and I wanted to take her somewhere nice. She's incredible and so beautiful...'

It appeared not to have occurred to Paul that it would suit his mistress if his wife found out and Paul was pushed to make a choice. She must be very confident, Cesare realised.

Backed up against his car, Cesare had adopted a folded-arm stance. It cut down on the temptation to grab his friend by the throat and demand to know what the hell he thought he was playing at, while Paul had given in to the need to unburden himself.

The less Cesare had said, the more Paul had confided in way too much detail. Reading between the lines a picture did emerge and it was a pattern Cesare recognised only too well.

The woman didn't just know what she was doing in the bedroom—again too much detail—she knew how to manipulate a man by recognising his weaknesses. She had flattered Paul, appealed to his vanity and managed to cleverly awaken his protective instincts.

Cesare was sure that this was a technique she would refine over the years, perhaps becoming as skilled as his own mother, who he had watched work her way across Europe leaving a trail of broken-hearted men in her wake.

'What would you do if you were me?'

The appeal had irritated Cesare, who could not by any stretch of the imagination imagine himself in a similar situation. For starters he had no plans to marry—ever—but he could see that marriage suited some men and Paul was one of them.

'I am not you. I thought you and Clare were happy.'

'We are.'

'And you love her?'

'I love them both, of course I do, but Rosie is so… She needs me. If I finished with her it would kill her. She loves me!'

Cesare, who had no taste for drama, had taken this statement with a pinch of salt. His indifference to the feelings or threats of a woman who had embarked on an affair with a married man remained, but, recalling that he had only just resisted the impulse to tell his friend to grow a pair, Cesare felt a stab of guilt.

It was easy to be contemptuous when you hadn't been close enough to feel the sensuality this woman projected. Her mouth was nothing short of sinful. The full pink curves promising passion to those lucky enough to taste them. As his sympathy for his friend grew so did his distaste for this woman who used her sensuality as a weapon.

'I will not keep you long, Miss Henderson. Would you like to take a seat?'

As no was not an option Anna did so, very aware of the critical, unfriendly eyes that followed her every move.

'Miss Henderson travelled up last night on the sleeper train. She must be tired,' the fatherly local councillor remarked before retaking his seat.

'You are seeing us at our best. The winter is a long one.'

The inference being presumably that she'd burst into tears at the sight of a snowflake. This from someone who looked as if he'd seen a hell of a lot more sun than she had. And an incomer to boot!

'Have you lived here long, Mr Urquart?'

Anna was aware of amused glances passing between the other members of the panel. What had she said that was so funny?

'All my life.'

It was the woman on the panel who explained the joke. 'The Urquarts of Killaran have historically been generous benefactors to the community and Cesare makes time in his crowded schedule to act as a school governor.'

Anna watched under the shield of her lashes as he sketched a quick smile; he was hard not to watch. His voice too was memorable, deep and velvety with a hint of gravel but no sign of a Highland lilt despite all this Urquart of Killaran stuff. Did that make him a laird or something? It would explain his warm reception, though such a thing as a laird, especially one who looked more like her private image of a pirate, seemed wildly anachronistic to Anna.

What would he look like in a kilt? She managed to swallow the inappropriate giggle produced by the equally inappropriate thought and lowered her lashes.

Always assuming her instincts were right and she had the job, did that mean she'd be working closely with him?

The thought made her heart beat even faster. With luck he kept his involvement to cheque book.

She struggled not to flinch as his attention swivelled back to her. The recognition she had thought she'd glimpsed initially was gone, replaced by a flat look that she could not read. Even so, she felt her anxiety levels climb—as it turned out with good reason!

'So tell me how long have you been teaching?'

'Five, no four...'

His intense gaze brought a rush of colour to her cheeks, one of the curses of her red-haired complexion. She managed to retain a semblance of what she hoped came across as headmistress-style gravity as she tipped her head. 'Five and a half years.'

Cesare Urquart, his elbows on the table, leaned forward across the table towards her. The undercurrent swirling behind his smooth smile made Anna feel a lot like Little Red Riding Hood. The man made your average wolf seem benevolent.

'Let me give you a hypothetical situation, Miss Henderson.'

Anna smiled back and nodded. Bring it on.

CHAPTER TWO

Pride alone kept Anna's shoulders straight and her head high as she left the room, pausing to nod and murmur a thank you to the panel members. Pride, and a grim teeth-clenching determination not to give Cesare Urquart the pleasure of seeing her crumble.

He didn't avoid her eyes or attempt to hide the smug smile with the hint of chilling cruelty that pulled the corners of his sensually sculpted mouth upwards. His complacent expression said job well done. The other panel members remained silent, none met her eyes, which was probably just as well as a word of kindness and she would have fallen apart.

'I'll call you a taxi.'

This offer definitely wasn't a kindness so Anna was able to hold it together as she met the stare of her tormentor. Hold it together but not conceal the bewildered hurt in her blue eyes.

He was the first to lower his gaze, his dark, preposterously long spiky lashes casting a shadow along the razor-sharp edge of his chiselled cheekbones as he picked up his pen, twirling it between long brown fingers before he scribbled something on the sheet of paper that lay on the table, drawing a line figuratively and literally through her name, she speculated bitterly.

Why had he done it?

Just because he could?

Why had she let him?

In the corridor her courage deserted her and Anna slumped like a puppet whose strings had been cut, clutching her head. She had the beginning of a first-class migraine. She leaned heavily against the wall feeling the cold of the ugly green tiles through her thin jacket.

Her coat lay folded across the chair in the room she had just left, but pneumonia was an infinitely more attractive option than going back for it.

The loud tick of the clock on the wall opposite brought her dazed glance to the large clock. Her eyes widened. It had only been five minutes since she had stood there on the brink of being offered her dream job. It had taken Cesare Urquart less than five minutes to make her appear an incompetent idiot.

Five minutes to reduce her to a stuttering level of incompetence, and she had let him! With a grimace of self-disgust, she straightened up and began to walk down the corridor, her heels beating out an angry tattoo.

The taxi was waiting for her outside. As she slid inside she could think of any number of responses to his seemingly innocent questions. He'd led her to the edge of a hole but she'd jumped in. And he'd enjoyed it!

A person who stubbornly clung to the belief that people were basically good, Anna didn't want to believe that he'd taken pleasure from her distress. But it was true, and probably the worst part of it was the knowledge that behind the bland and beautiful mask he had enjoyed watching her stutter and stumble. It had been clinical and cruel.

She looked at her hands. They were shaking. She made a decision. They'd arrived at her hotel.

'Do you mind waiting?' There was no way she was safe to drive her hire car the forty miles back to Inverness. She didn't actually care what the taxi there cost her: it would be worth it not to stay another second.

Having reassured the car-hire firm she would be happy to pay the supplementary charge for them to pick up the car, Anna packed her bag in about thirty seconds. She was booked into the hotel overlooking the picturesque working harbour for two nights, but the view had lost its charm, as had the Highlands.

The thought of all things familiar and safe made her chest ache with longing. Everyone had been right. Moving up here had been a stupid idea, not because, as Rosie had suggested, there were no men—that was fine by Anna—but because there was one man. A man she could not even think about without wanting to break things. His head would be a good start.

She climbed back into the taxi. She fastened her seat belt and closed the door with a restrained bang. 'Inverness station, please.'

Anna was actually in her seat on the train when all passengers were asked to disembark. No trains were running on the line between Inverness and Glasgow due to flooding and stormy weather further down the line.

'Hail the size of golf balls, they say.'

Those passengers who requested details of bus times were told that bus drivers too were not risking the journey.

Anna normally maintained a philosophical frame of mind when events were out of her control, but if ever there was a day to respond with anger and frustration this was it.

Could this day get any worse?

Of course it could. This was the day that just kept giving and the man who just kept appearing. Twice was not a lot but it felt like more.

The gleaming car Cesare Urquart stood beside did not suggest he came under the category of traditional impoverished laird. It did not come as a surprise to Anna that having money would be the way he got away with being so totally obnoxious.

Human nature being what it was, people were prepared to put up with a lot from people who held the purse strings and the power. And what Cesare had done to her was a classic case of an abuse of power. It was inexplicable to Anna, who hated to see anyone unhappy, that a person could take such malicious pleasure out of causing someone pain, presumably just because he could.

Yet it had felt personal, very personal. That continued to bemuse her; if the man hadn't been a total stranger she'd have felt the interview had been payback of some sort. Perhaps, she brooded bitterly, he took offence to redheads, who in her opinion got a bad press. Her temper was no fierier than anyone else's. She pressed her fingers to her drumming temples. She actually considered herself to have quite a placid personality.

As was appropriate, Cesare had paused to congratulate the successful candidate after the interviews finished. The choice had not seemed difficult to him yet some of the panel had agonised over it and in the end the final decision had not been unanimous, even after a few probing questions where the redhead had become almost incoherent.

An image of those big, hurt, cobalt-blue eyes formed in his head and he firmly pushed it away. He was sure that the formula had been working all of her life. One look at those expressive eyes…a suggestion of tears bravely blinked away while she channelled inner integrity…had made his jaw tighten. The panel members, who had still stood by their original choice, would have been less disgruntled if they knew what he knew about Miss Henderson.

'So you think it's a good idea to build an office block on the lawn after we've bulldozed the—'

Cesare turned his attention to his sister. 'Fine… fine…'

Her musical laughter drew several stares but then his model sister generally did draw stares.

'What?' he asked irritably.

'You haven't been listening to a word I've said.'

He flashed her an impatient glance and opened the passenger door. 'Just get in, will you?'

Her delicate brows lifted. 'You're in a foul mood, I get that, but don't take it out on me, big brother,' she advised.

Cesare scowled at the suggestion and bit back. 'I am not in a foul mood.' His conscience was clear when the welfare of impressionable children was at stake. You didn't give anyone the benefit of the doubt and there was no doubt.

This time his sister's laughter was drowned out by another loudspeaker announcement explaining once more that, due to flooding on the line, the Edinburgh trains were cancelled. Not good news for the stranded passengers who had began to troop with varying degrees of resignation from the station.

'Lucky I decided to catch the early train,' Angel observed.

In her thin jacket Anna shivered, her throat tightened until she could hardly breathe. The booming noise in her head got louder and louder as she continued to stare at him, standing there as if he owned the place, not getting out of the way because he expected other people to...and they did. He was getting in the way and they were apologising for bumping into him.

And she'd done the same, though in her case it was not just walk around him—she'd let him walk all over her! She had just sat there and taken what he'd dished out during that interview. It was not her finest hour.

If she'd told him what she thought of him she knew she wouldn't be feeling this awful, instead she felt...

'Pathetic!' she exclaimed to the world in general.

'Are you all right, dear?'

Responding with a forced smile and an embarrassed laugh for the benefit of the concerned elderly couple who had approached her, Anna nodded and lied. 'Yes, fine, I'm...'

Her voice trailed away and her smile vanished as a tall, hateful figure placed a hand on his beautiful companion's elbow.

She inhaled and squeezed her eyes closed. Now was her chance to tell him what she really thought of him. She nodded to the couple, lifted her stuffed overnight bag and propelled herself through the crowds.

'I expected you to bring Jas. Is she all right?'

As his sister looked around as though expecting her daughter to materialise, Cesare opened the passenger door. 'She's fine,' he soothed. 'I came straight from the school interviews for the new head.'

'Many candidates?' Angel glanced down at the file that lay open on the passenger seat and paused, glancing down at the name on the front page. 'More than one, I hope.'

'More than one,' her brother agreed. Snatching the CV from her fingers, he flung it onto the back seat, consigning it and the person who had supplied it to a dark corner.

His sister made no attempt to get in the car. She was studying his face. 'You look strange. Are you sure Jas is all right—nothing's happened?'

'A man could be excused for thinking you don't think he's capable of looking after a five-year-old.' Despite his comment Cesare didn't take her anxiety personally. He knew how hard it was for his sister to delegate any responsibility where her daughter was concerned, and he also knew he was a poor substitute for her absentee nanny who had broken her leg. Fortunately the injury would not put her out of action for as long as his niece had been with the painful hip complaint, Perthes, that had confined her to bed rest for weeks.

'I know Jas is a full-time job and she can twist you around her little finger. How did the physio go this week? Did she play up? I hope you remembered—'

His sister's voice faded as among the stream of frustrated travellers streaming out of the station, one caught his eye.

The amazing copper-coloured hair made her stand out like a flash of colour in a monochrome picture. Her blue eyes fixed on his face and she was heading his way like some sort of petite avenging angel. All the image lacked was a blazing sword, which was just as well because she looked as if she'd happily have skewered him if she'd had anything sharp to hand.

Conscious of a buzz of anticipation, he waited. He had not sought this encounter but he was not going to avoid it. As she got closer he felt the faint nagging guilt that he had been unwilling to acknowledge dissolve. The woman approaching was not the defeated, dejected figure who more resembled a mistreated kitten than a seasoned seductress. This was a sexy, smouldering redhead who moved with supple feline grace. The woman who would have caused havoc in the small community.

The muscles along his jaw tightened as she turned to heave the bag she was half dragging onto her shoulder, giving him an excellent, if fleeting, view of her taut, rounded behind. If he had needed proof of the walking danger she represented to men it was provided by the scorching flash of heat that sizzled through his own body to settle in his groin. If running true to form she would have worked her way through the married men in the area in a couple of months!

'Someone you know?' Angel murmured, looking curiously from her brother, who had frozen to the spot, to the slim, flame-haired figure approaching them as fast as the bag she was lugging would allow.

'Stay out of this, Angel.'

Anna, close enough to hear this terse aside, didn't know who she felt more scornful towards. Him, for speaking that way, or the woman for tolerating it.

Anna's glance slid over Cesare Urquart's predictably glamorous companion, a tall, utterly stunning brunette, made taller by the crazy spiky heels she was wearing, which she'd teamed with a retro-styled tea dress and a leather biker jacket. A challenging combination that she managed to carry off with style.

Pulling herself up to her full five feet three, Anna halted and, breathing hard, levelled an accusing finger at Cesare's broad chest. She was struggling to articulate her fury, so she stuttered. 'Y-you!'

His right eyebrow hitched a little higher as he tipped his head. 'Miss Henderson?'

Previously his hostility had been masked, now it was overt. Her inarticulate fury gave way to bewilderment.

'Look, you're a bully, I get that, but what I would like to know is why?'

'You are a bad loser, Miss Henderson.'

She lifted her chin and declared proudly, 'But an excellent teacher.'

The furrow between his brows deepened as she wrapped her arms around herself, but carried on shivering.

'Why have you not got a coat on?' he demanded irritably.

The question briefly threw Anna off her stride. 'I lost it,' she snarled through gritted teeth.

'Why?' she repeated, her militant attitude giving way to genuine confusion. It was utterly impossible for soft-hearted Anna, who would not have deliberately set out to injure her worst enemy, let alone a total stranger, to understand how or why someone would do what he had.

'It was my job to ensure that the school has the best possible head, and you were simply not up to the job.' He curved his fingers around the beautiful brunette's elbow. 'If you'll excuse me.'

The dismissal relit the smouldering flames of Anna's fury. 'No, I won't!' she cried, catching his arm.

He swung back, his metallic stare conveying astonishment before it moved with significance to the small white hand against his sleeve.

Anna's hand fell self-consciously away, her nerve endings still retaining the impression of hard muscle even after she rubbed her hand against her thigh. 'There is something else—I know there is.'

He arched a sardonic brow. 'Beyond your incompetence?'

'The others thought I was competent. I am competent,' she qualified angrily as her fingers itched to slap the contemptuous smile off his hatefully perfect face.

'Until you arrived, the panel thought I was the right person for the job.'

His lip curled. 'On paper you looked an adequate candidate.'

The comment sent his sister's interested glance to the file her brother had flung onto the back seat.

'Adequate?' Anna growled.

Cesare dragged his gaze up from the full pouting curve of her lush lips, where it kept sliding. 'I am sure you are accustomed to smiling and getting your own way. Being born beautiful does not grant you special privileges in life, Miss Henderson.'

Anna blinked. Beautiful? She half expected to see sarcasm in his stare, but she saw only anger and something she struggled to put a name to. The indefinable dark something made her stomach muscles quiver.

She wasn't beautiful.

'For a moment I thought you were Rosie.'

Anna had lost count of the number of times she had heard that comment while she was growing up and she understood it: her older cousin, whom she admired and loved, was beautiful.

It was a subtle thing, beauty. She was Rosanna, though she much preferred to be called Anna. She had freckles, with a not quite straight nose and a mouth that was too wide. She was okay-looking whereas Rosemary was stunning. Her cousin could have had any man; instead she had fallen for the creep who had very nearly ruined her life.

'If anyone here is privileged...' She gave a scornful hoot of laughter. 'You know what I think? I think you like to prove what a big man you are because you're not—what you are is a bully, a pathetic bully.' He looked so astonished she almost laughed. 'What do you do as an encore? Kick puppies?'

'I hardly think the analogy is apt, Miss Henderson.' Not a puppy, but there was definitely something feline about this sexy red-headed witch.

She gave a cranky grunt and snarled through clenched teeth, 'Will you stop calling me that?'

'Would you prefer Rosie?'

She blinked. It was weird to hear this man call her by her cousin's diminutive. 'My name is Rosanna.' It didn't really matter what he called her because he'd always manage to make it sound like an insult. 'My friends.' She gulped, suddenly feeling very far away from those friends. 'They call me A-Anna.'

Was this display of quivering bravery meant to make him feel guilty? 'Have you ever heard the phrase what goes around comes around, Miss Henderson?'

'If that were true something large would fall from the sky and hit you on your fat, self-important head!'

The snort of laughter drew Anna's attention to the beautiful brunette, who rather unexpectedly grinned at her in an encouraging way and gave a thumbs-up sign.

Cesare flashed his sister a look without having any real expectation of it having any effect, then returned his attention to the slim redhead who, when she wasn't abusing him, was playing for the sympathy vote.

'Do you mind lowering your voice?'

She adopted a puzzled expression. 'Why? It can't be a secret you're a cold-hearted bully.'

His silver-grey eyes narrowed to slits at the jibe. 'We can trade insults if you wish.' His smile suggested he thought he'd come off better in this exchange. 'What do you call a woman who targets married men?'

Anna's jaw dropped. 'What?'

'Paul Dane is a good friend of mine.'

The name caused the blood to drain out of Anna's face, leaving her marble pale as the day's events clicked into place. Suddenly it all made sickening sense. This man thought she was Rosie!

'Suddenly you have less to say.'

Her eyes blinked wide open. Not, as he anticipated, filled with the shame of discovery, but angry. Sparkling like blue sapphires. His contemptuous smile faded as a furrow formed between his darkly defined brows.

Of course, this man and Paul Dane were friends. 'A marriage made in heaven,' she murmured.

'Paul's marriage is still strong, despite your efforts to end it.'

'My efforts?' She shook her head, her chest dramatically lifting as she struggled to control her feelings. 'Sorry, did I get that right? You think your friend Paul is some sort of a victim?' Anna began to laugh, her anger growing cold. It had taken her cousin a very long time to recover from the affair with the married man who had broken her heart. Rosie, whose only sin had been that she was too loving and trusting, that she followed her heart.

And she was brave too. A lesser person would have been destroyed by what had happened, but not Rosie. Anna's admiration for her gutsy cousin was tinged with

worry. Yes, Rosie had found her happy-ever-after sce-
nario, but following her heart could just as easily have
led to another heartbreak, another Paul Dane.

Rosie had taken the risk but even the thought of following her example was enough to send a ripple of horror through Anna. The nightmares of the night she had
discovered her cousin semi-conscious beside a half-
empty bottle of pills and a bottle of booze were less
frequent now, but they still came. If one positive thing
had come from that experience it was the knowledge
that she would never allow her heart to rule her head.

Her expression sobered as she angled a scorn-filled
look up at his dark lean face. So certain, so superior!
She gave a snort of disgust. 'Stupid question, of course
you do.'

'Paul was not without blame,' he conceded, slinging
her an impatient look.

'Big of you to say so.' She tilted her head back to
direct a contemptuous look at his face. 'This is how I
know it to be. A man, a *married* man who seduces an
inexperienced, starry-eyed girl ten years his junior, a
man who tells her he loves her and is going to leave
his wife for her.'

Too furious to consider her words, she gave a bitter laugh and added, 'Yes, the girl knows she is doing
wrong.' An image of Rosie's tear-stained face as she
clutched that bottle of pills flashed into Anna's head
as she relived that awful moment.

'But she does it anyway,' Anna finished in a voice
husky with emotion. 'She lies to her family and when
he dumps her and goes back to his wife she thinks her

life is over. I'm not sure what I'd call a man like that but it sure as hell wouldn't be victim!'

At least she had stopped short of revealing the whole story. Even so, Anna immediately felt guilty and disloyal. She had promised Rosie never to reveal what she knew to anyone, it was a promise that up to this point she had honoured.

The only comfort was that this man thought she was the person who had fallen victim to his friend and while she hated being thought of as this naïve victim, it was preferable to having this man sneer at Rosie, judge her.

Let him think what he liked about her. Anna was more than willing to take one for the team if it meant protecting Rosie from his sneers and accusations.

Her passion caused the permanent indentation between Cesare's ebony brows to form into a V of doubt, which quickly smoothed. He resented the fact that this woman had made him even briefly doubt a man who had literally saved his life. He realised that she'd probably told this version of events so often that she believed it. A lot easier to believe a lie than admit you'd targeted a married man and relentlessly pursued him.

While Cesare didn't consider himself intolerant of weakness—he had enough of his own—when it came to the subject of fidelity within marriage there were no grey areas. It was simple: you stayed faithful or you didn't exchange vows you were not able to keep. This was the reason that he did not plan to take the marriage route. Loving the same woman for a lifetime or even a year? Impossible. Lying was a strong word even when the lie in question was directed to yourself. Did people, intelligent people, really believe it?

He gave a mental shrug. Maybe he was just wired differently? But for his money the existence of the Easter Bunny was easier to buy into than this soul-mate stuff. Sure, you grew comfortable over the years but who wanted to be comfortable when you could have passion and fire?

However, if you went down the marriage route, straying was not an option. It was true that Paul had not behaved well, but at least he'd come to his senses in time to save his marriage. Basically, Paul was one of life's good guys, capable of selfless acts. If he hadn't been Cesare knew he wouldn't be standing here now—Paul's selfless act had saved his skin.

'Get in the car, Angel,' he snapped at his companion before turning on his heel and presenting Anna with his broad-shouldered back.

Infuriated by the dismissal, Anna surged forward. The hasty action took her close to the edge of the pavement just as a bus drove by, depositing the contents of a deep puddle down the front of her suit.

'He didn't even slow down,' she wailed, looking from her dripping muddied front to the bus that was picking up speed as it continued down the road.

Just before he slid into the high-powered car beside his beautiful companion, Cesare Urquart turned his head. He didn't say a word, just looked her up and down and then smiled. Hateful, hateful man!

CHAPTER THREE

ANGEL SMOOTHED THE pages she had retrieved from the back seat. 'So that was Miss Henderson?' She tapped the typed name on the page before flashing a look at her brother. 'I take it she didn't get the job? Pity—anyone that gives as good as she gets with you might be just what we need.'

'That is private, Angel,' her brother snarled.

Angel read one of the attached references. 'It says here she has a natural empathy with children and she's—'

Cesare, making an effort to slow his breathing, interrupted irritably. 'Yeah, I know, she's perfect.'

A thoughtful expression crossed his sister's face. 'You know, I think she might be...'

'Put that down, Angel.' He clenched his teeth as his sister predictably tuned him out and turned another page.

'I'm curious,' she admitted, still skimming the page. 'Who was better than her?'

'Paper qualifications are all well and good.'

'You mean she's another one of Paul's victims.'

'What the hell do you mean by "another"?'

'I mean if you've got a blind spot it comes to that man. Don't look like that. I love Paul, he's a total charmer but, let's face it he's—'

Without warning Cesare pulled the car to the side of the road, drawing a startled gasp from his sister.

'Are you trying to tell me he made a pass at you?'

Reassured by his sister's peal of laughter enough to start breathing again, he released a deep sigh and turned the engine back on.

They had travelled a silent mile before Angel voiced the question she already knew the answer to. 'And if he had?'

'I'd kill him,' Cesare informed her, with a total lack of emotion.

His response told Angel nothing she didn't already know. 'So saving your life makes it all right for him to mess with the—' she wafted the printed CV his way '—Miss Hendersons of the world, but not your sister?'

'Shut up, Angel.'

Smiling, she licked her finger and chalked up an invisible point in the air, drawing an almost smile from her grim-faced brother before she began to read the CV, which described the sort of person who even the most paranoid parent would feel happy about leaving in charge of their child.

'Hi...Anna?'

Anna, who was on the point of leaving, turned and saw the beautiful brunette who had been with Cesare Urquart standing in the doorway of the hotel room she had been forced to take for the night. This morning the brunette was wearing jeans tucked into a pair of knee-high boots and a short fur-collared leather jacket, her river-straight, silky, waist-length jet-black hair secured in a ponytail at the nape of her neck. Even if Anna hadn't been having a bad hair day, and she really was, the woman would have made her feel hopelessly inadequate.

'I don't think your boyfriend will like it if you're seen talking to me.'

Angel scowled. 'I don't care much what Cesare likes.'

Her brother had not reacted well to her suggestion over breakfast that his attitude to this woman was coloured by their own mother, and even less well when she had said that just because someone saved your life it didn't mean they were a saint. And when she'd mentioned her totally brilliant idea he had suggested she had lost her mind.

'And he's not my boyfriend, he's my brother.'

Anna's chin dropped from the defiant angle as her eyes widened. 'Brother!' Were the whole family this stunning?

Anna's shocked exclamation drew a grin.

'I'd like to say he got the looks and I got the brains but I'd be lying.' Her expression sobered. 'But brainy or not, Cesare can be pretty stupid sometimes and he's pathologically loyal to his friends even the ones who haven't...' She broke off, giving the impression of someone biting their tongue. 'And, of course, sorry doesn't come easy to him.'

Anna gave an unamused snort. The idea of that hateful man wanting to apologise was a joke. None of this was his sister's fault so she forced a faint smile, but was unable to bite back her bitter retort. 'Especially as he's always right.'

The willowy brunette winced. 'Ouch! So you are heading back to...London?'

Anna glanced at her watch. The information she'd received advised that passengers should only travel if their journey was strictly necessary because there were still flood warnings, and though some trains were running today there were numerous delays. The likelihood was her journey would take a lot longer than normal. At best, according to her enquiries, the trains were running on average three hours behind schedule.

'I haven't much reason to hang around.'

'I suppose you have plans for your summer break.'

The seemingly casual remark drew a sigh from Anna. Break? Her summer break might end up being longer than she would have liked. Still, she'd done stints of supply teaching before and she could again.

'Is there something I can help you with, Miss Urquart?'

'It's Angel and, yes, there is. When is your train due? Do you have time for a coffee? The place on the corner is actually pretty good.'

Her last phone call to the help line had suggested she had time for a three-course banquet but she shook her head in a negative motion. Despite her refusal she was actually rather intrigued by this woman's appearance.

'Sorry.'

'You're probably wondering what I want?'

'I'm curious,' Anna admitted.

'I have a daughter.' She waved her ring hand at Anna. 'And, no, I'm not married.'

Half the children in her class of thirty in the inner-city school where Anna had worked had come from single-parent backgrounds.

'And I never have been. Jas…Jasmine is a great kid. I just wish I could spend more time with her. It's hard juggling.' The frown on her brow smoothed as she added, 'I'm luckier than most because my work is more flexible. Normally I keep the holidays free and, of course, Cesare is great but obviously he can't be here all the time. He's a victim of his own success.' She looked at Anna and, after receiving a blank look back, loosed an incredulous laugh. 'You've no idea who he is, do you?'

'I know what he is…' Anna gave a shamed grimace and grunted. 'Sorry, he's your brother.'

Angel looked amused. 'Oh, don't hold back on my account. Cesare can look after himself.'

'I know your family owns the estate and castle. I suppose that makes him pretty important.' In his own eyes at least, she thought viciously. 'Locally.'

'Sure, the Urquarts have been here for ever, but the estate barely breaks even. It'll be years before it does despite the money he's poured in over the last five years. Dad, bless him, was pretty resistant to change and Mum, before she packed her bags, was terribly expensive. Her divorce settlement was pretty extreme. Anyway, I digress. You don't want to know about the family,'

On the contrary, Anna was eating up every fascinating detail.

'I take it you're not a fan of Formula One racing?' Angel continued.

'Not my thing.'

Was Cesare some kind of racing-car driver? It figured.

Danger and glamour plus a ridiculous amount of adulation—yes, she could see that suiting him.

'Well, actually he is what most people would call famous.' Accustomed to seeing her brother the target of women who had been known to stalk him in packs, Angel was amused that this girl didn't have a clue who he was.

'He was champion driver two years running.' Anna watched a shadow cross the other girl's beautiful face before she adopted a brisk tone and explained, 'Obviously that was before the crash, then he moved seamlessly into management and took over team Romero.'

A crash! News reports of crashes always made Anna leave the room or switch channel; now the word made her shudder.

'Was he...?' She stopped. Presumably he had been injured, but if he bore any scars Anna hadn't seen any—not that she had seen that much of him. Without warning an image floated before her eyes—a pretty detailed image.

Wafting cold air on her face with her hand, she cleared her throat more successfully than she cleared her mind of a naked bronzed man. 'Romero?' Even she had heard of the famous Italian racing team. 'So he doesn't live here?'

'The team is based in Italy but after Dad died Cesare

made the decision to live here. Obviously he travels a lot.' She grimaced. 'We both do—pretty ironic considering how we both hated it when we were kids. Our mum got custody after the divorce,' she explained. 'And she has what you could call a low boredom threshold— she doesn't stay in one place for long.'

She flashed Anna a wry smile. 'So neither did we. When Jas was born I was determined that she had security, stability, a stable home life.'

The implication that she, and presumably her brother, had not enjoyed this sort of childhood was not lost on Anna who felt a stab of sympathy. Not for Cesare, obviously, but for this beautiful young woman. Anna might have been tragically orphaned, not what most people would call a perfect childhood, but after her parents' death she had been raised in a warm and loving home and treated as much a daughter as Rosie by her aunt and uncle.

'I always feel guilty when I go away for work but...' Angel shook her head. 'I wish now I'd not taken this job. It's too big a commitment.' Anna, who had seen that look of guilt on the face of many working mothers trying to juggle childcare, struggled to maintain her detachment. Giving full rein to her empathy had led in the past to Anna being taken advantage of—it wasn't going to happen again. She'd toughened up. Watching the person you loved most in the whole world having her stomach pumped did that to a person.

'I hadn't worked for three months while Jas was ill and in my business people have short memories. You're only as good as your last assignment. I thought it might be tough to… Well, anyway, when I got offered this Face of Floriel gig I just grabbed it, but then—' she sighed '—not thinking of consequences is the story of my life.'

Anna felt a flash of something close to envy. Had she ever done anything without thinking of consequences? Her caution was probably why everyone had considered it wildly out of character when she had gone for a job outside the city she'd lived in for most of her life.

'Look, I wish I could help.' She liked Angel Urquart and she would have liked to help her out.

Do not go there, Anna. Don't even think it.

'You can.'

Anna shook her head. 'You must see that's impossible. Obviously I'm very sorry your daughter has been ill—'

'She missed all of last term.'

'I'm sure she'll catch up quickly. They do at that age.' Anna stopped as things suddenly clicked into place in her head.

'Oh, wow, you're that model…Angel.' Minus dramatic make-up, this was the woman with the impossibly perfect body, the woman from the ad campaign advertising lingerie. The images were plastered on the side of every bus in London a year or so ago.

'Right now I'm the mum Angel and I just know that this will work. And you wouldn't have to worry about Cesare,' she cut in quickly. 'It's a very big castle. Jas and I have an apartment in the west wing so we're totally independent. Of course, he'd be there if you needed him.'

Needing Cesare Urquart? 'I won't.'

'Then you'll do it?'

Anna's eyes widened in dismay. 'No, I just meant… Does he…?' She swallowed, unable to bring herself to say the name of the man. 'Does your brother know you're here?'

'I mentioned it.'

Anna's lips twisted in a dubious smile. She was not fooled for a second by the casual tone. 'And he's willing to run the risk of me contaminating your daughter?' Anna couldn't keep the bitterness from her voice.

Angel laid her hand on Anna's shoulder. She was smiling but her narrowed green eyes shone with determination. 'Cesare is my brother and I owe him a lot, but I'm Jas's mother and where her welfare is concerned I make the decisions.'

'But if you work, don't you already have childcare?'

'Sure, Jas has a nanny, only poor Jenny came off her bike, broke her leg and won't be out of her plaster for another six weeks. She'd hobble back to work if I let her, but it's out of the question.' She gave a sigh. 'Look, forget it. This isn't your problem. I shouldn't have come, and believe me you're not the only one who is intimidated by my big brother.' She fastened the button on her jacket and swept a strand of gleaming dark hair from her face.

'I'm not intimidated by your brother.'

'Of course you're not,' Angel soothed.

Anna's jaw tightened. 'I'll do it.'

Angel's smile flashed. She was already fishing a mobile phone from her pocket. 'Are you sure?'

'Totally.'

Angel made a call on her mobile.

'Hi, Hamish. Yes. Bring Jas up.' She looked at the bag on Anna's bed. 'Good, you're packed,' she approved. 'You travel light, but no problem—we can stop on the way and pick up some more things. What size are you—six, eight?'

Anna blinked. 'Your daughter is here? You expect me to come now?'

Angel looked surprised by the question. 'Anna, I'm catching my flight at midnight and—'

'You must have been very sure I'd say yes.'

The woman gave an airy shrug. 'I'm by nature an optimistic person.'

Anna gave the sleek, stylish brunette a long searching look. Before she could challenge Angel, the door burst open and a small dark-haired figure burst in. Jas Urquart had a shy version of her mother's smile and a front tooth missing. She was the embodiment of heartbreakingly adorable.

CHAPTER FOUR

HAD SHE BEEN down this corridor before? Anna looked around, trying to decide if the tapestry on the wall looked familiar. She shook her head in defeat; she didn't have a clue. She kicked herself for not paying more attention.

Instead of looking for landmarks, Anna had been listening to Jasmine's stream of chatter as the lively little girl had skipped along beside her, relaying some gruesome history, or possibly fantasy—the child clearly had a very lively imagination—of the castle that was her home.

The childish confidences had been liberally littered with her uncle's name. Based on her experience, Anna would have thought he would feature as an ogre in a child's life, but no, it was clear that for Jas at least he was something of a hero, endowed, if she was to be believed, with superhuman skills.

Oh, well, I'm sure he'd be the first to agree, Anna thought as her stomach muscles reacted to the image that floated into her head. Eyes as hard and cold as polished steel, a mouth that was cruel. A mouth that was…

She lifted a hand to one warm cheek and, sucking

in air through flared nostrils, attempted to banish the image.

'You've done what?'

Had she conjured Cesare up from her fevered imagination? This place was huge—how was it that she couldn't avoid him, ever?

'I thought we agreed.' He was heading towards her, arguing furiously with Angel.

Shaking free of the frozen horror that had nailed her to the spot, Anna stepped back into the shadows. It wasn't just the three sets of stone steps she had jogged up and down that made her heart pound in her chest as she shamelessly eavesdropped...short of covering her ears, what choice did she have?

When she responded, Angel's voice did not suggest she was intimidated by the outrage in her brother's voice; she sounded faintly amused. But mingled with the amusement was a hint of steely determination. Anna's admiration for her employer went even higher. It took someone with guts to stand up to Cesare Urquart.

'You talked, I listened and then I asked Anna Henderson to stay until term starts. She can tutor Jas and help her catch up with the work she missed, and be there to care for her when I'm away.'

'There must be an alternative. I'll speak to the agency.'

'Sure, and they'll send some girl who'll spend more time flirting with you than taking care of Jas. It's not your fault you're eye candy, darling brother, but Anna is perfect. She doesn't like you.

'This woman—'

'Look, Cesare, before you start you have a problem with Anna. I don't. I know that Paul can do no wrong in your eyes and that's fine, you can be in his debt for ever if you like, but he's human and people make mistakes. Just look at me.'

'This woman is nothing like you.'

'No. she didn't get pregnant. It's daft to assume that it was all her fault. You want to know what I think?'

'No.'

'Fine,' came the easy reply. 'I have to be away for the next month. It's not perfect, I know, but then, well, bottom line is, there's nothing I can do about it, and with Anna—'

'You don't have to work.'

'And you don't have to be a serial seducer but you are. Sorry, but I'm not about to sponge off my big brother.'

'There is no question of sponging, Angel.' Anna could hear the irritation in his voice. She gave a contemptuous grimace. The man had the sensitivity of a brick. He should be admiring his sister for wanting to be independent, not knocking her. 'This is about Jasmine, not your pride.'

'Don't try and emotionally blackmail me. This isn't about me, is it? This woman really has got under your skin, hasn't she?'

Have I? Anna thought from her hiding place.

'But you're right, this is about what's best for Jas. I'm sorry if you don't like it but she stays, and for God's sake be nice to her.'

His response was a deep mumble that Anna didn't catch. She shouldn't be eavesdropping! She felt a belated stab of guilt. She ought to reveal herself, she knew she should, it was the right thing to do. You are a coward, Anna Henderson, she told herself in disgust as she stayed where she was.

'You're just going to have to suck it up, big brother.'

There followed another angry exchange, this time in Italian, before Anna heard a female laugh followed by the sound of heels vanishing in the opposite direction. The other, heavier, footsteps got closer…oh, help!

Anna was faced with the choice to hide in the shadows and hope he didn't see her or reveal herself.

Had Anna got under his skin? The lines bracketing his sensual mouth deepened as, ebony brows drawn into a scowling straight line above his masterful nose, Cesare turned the words over in his head. It was true. The redhead *had* got under his skin.

An image of her soft mouth and extraordinary luminous sky-blue eyes floated into his head. His lips tightened as he banished it, aware as he did so that it was not likely to stay banished. For a man who took his self-control pretty much for granted, this knowledge was an added irritant. He had only encountered the woman a mere twenty-four hours ago and in that time she had rarely been out of his thoughts. Take last night, for example. He shook his head slightly, dislodging the images, none innocent and all involving that lush mouth! She was going to be living under his roof so he needed to keep his imagination and his libido on a tight rein.

He recognised that the most irritating part of the situation was that his sister had made her argument pretty well, somehow giving the woman victim status, which was laughable. As for the implication that he was somehow prejudiced? He might be forced to accept the situation but he was not about to accept this skewed view, though he could see why it suited his sister. From her point of view this was an ideal solution to her short-term problem. Great for Angel, not so great for him bumping into a woman whom he despised and desired with equal force.

It was an admission, a weakness, he would never have needed to acknowledge if she and her red hair had simply left, but she hadn't and pretending a situation didn't exist was no defence. Face the problem and then deal with it.

Angel might trust her with Jasmine but he gave Miss Henderson two weeks tops before she stepped out of line, and when she did he'd be there.

Anna took a deep breath and stepped out in front of Cesare.

'S-sorry if I shouldn't be here but I think I got a bit turned around on the third staircase.' Her shaky laugh was met with stony silence.

Cesare felt a jolt of shock as the woman that he had mentally been cursing emerged from the shadows. Against the stone wall her face was a pale oval, the hair that had been a subject of unwilling fascination for him yesterday today hung loose and untamed, the rippling, richly coloured Pre-Raphaelite waves falling down her narrow back. Gone also was the professional suit, replaced today by a pair of faded jeans that clung to the slight feminine curve of her hips. Tucked into the belt cinched across her hips, the blue striped top echoed the cobalt colour of her eyes.

As he read the mixture of wariness and defiance in their jewelled depths along with the heat flash that consolidated in his aching groin he felt a fresh stab of belated empathy for his friend who had been unable to resist the lure of her lush mouth. Mingled in with the empathy was something that felt suspiciously like envy.

Anna attributed the acute and unpleasant dizziness that made her grip the rail of the gallery high above the baronial hall to vertigo.

Objectively she recognised that Cesare Urquart himself might cause many women to feel light-headed, but her only response was a prickle of antagonism and a relapse of the stuttering she had conquered years ago. She moistened her lips and struggled not to look like someone compounding trespass with eavesdropping. 'I'm not sure where I should be?'

In my bed.

For a split second the involuntary thought almost made it out of his mouth. His darkened eyes shuttered and the muscles in his brown throat worked hard as he fought to control the surge of testosterone-fuelled lust that continued to lick like a flame through his body.

The weakness irritated him. 'Where do you want to be?' he snapped.

Anywhere but here, she thought, wondering how she had ever allowed herself to be manoeuvred into taking this job. She should be back home looking for a proper job, getting herself signed up for relief work as a short-term measure. As for living under the same roof as a man who despised her almost as much as she despised him, what had she been thinking?

Her eyes slid across the strong bones of his dark patrician face. She might loathe him but that didn't make him any less attractive. Damn the man!

Anna knew she had to pull herself together.

If she'd vanished meekly, tail between her legs, she'd have been doing exactly what he wanted—also exactly what she wanted, but that wasn't the point.

So what was the point?

She wanted to help Angel, and why should the single mother trying to do a good job suffer because of who her brother was? She'd do this job so well, even if it killed her, that even Cesare would have to admit he had misjudged her. All at once her sense of realism intruded on this attractive flight of fancy.

In an alternate universe maybe Cesare Urquart would be overcome with remorse and regret when he realised that because of him the community had lost out on an exceptional head teacher, but in the real world the man was never ever going to admit he was wrong, even if his life depended on it.

She dragged her eyes, which had drifted down his body, up to face level. 'I was trying to find the door where I came in.'

One dark brow lifted, the eyes stayed dark and hostile. The aloof disdain she could only assume was permanent. 'You are leaving already?'

Don't get your hopes up, mate, she thought. 'When I commit to something I see it through.'

A spasm of annoyance crossed his lean face. 'How

admirable, always supposing that something isn't another woman's husband. I can only presume that you took this job as some sort of petty revenge to annoy me.'

'No, that wasn't the reason, but it is a plus,' she admitted, and had the satisfaction of seeing his jaw clench. 'I hate to break this to you but not everything is about you.' She bit her lip, regretting the words, not because of the flash of astonished anger in his face, but because there was no point winding him up while she was here. 'I took this job because...'

Good question.

Why had she taken this job?

'Well, how could I pass up the opportunity to see you every day and have one of our delightful discussions?'

From somewhere the memory surfaced of Rosie, months after the end of her affair, describing the physical craving she still felt to hear her lover's voice, to catch a glimpse of him even after all he had done to her. Made uneasy by the mental connection and wondering if wrapped up inside the layers of sarcasm there was even a thread of truth in her comment, Anna almost tipped over into outright panic...

She took a calming breath. She wasn't the craving kind, and if she was going to crave anyone or anything it wouldn't be this man!

He was everything she loathed. He was what she had vowed to protect herself from—the sort of man capable of inspiring obsession.

Recovering her poise, she met the sensational silvered gaze. All at once her precarious poise vanished.

Swallowing, Anna took an involuntary step backwards as he uncrossed one foot from the other and, his languid actions presenting a stark contrast to the gleam in his deep-set eyes, Cesare levered his broad shoulders from the wall where he had been leaning. As he peeled away the dark curve of lashes lifted off his chiselled cheekbones and she encountered the full force of the maliciously amused contempt in his eyes.

'Well, you'll have plenty of opportunity to see me.' He watched a spasm of wild-eyed panic cross her quite remarkably expressive face. For a woman who presumably had some experience in lying and cheating, she really did not hide her feelings well.

Promise, threat? She didn't want to know. 'I…I thought you travelled a great deal.'

He arched a sardonic brow. 'I am my own boss.'

'Nice for you. I'd settle for having a permanent job!' Anna flared back, taking refuge in resentment.

'Am I meant to feel guilty for your unemployment? If you resigned your post before you secured another you must have been very confident, or possibly,' he speculated nastily, 'you jumped before you were pushed?'

'I am confident that I am good at what I do,' she retorted with a quiet dignity that brought a frown to his face.

'But if you had bothered to read my CV you'd know that the inner-city school I was working at was a victim of closures.' It had been that circumstance and the encouragement of friends and colleagues, not ambition, that had made Anna apply for headships. She had been very happy where she was and being a deputy head had meant she'd still retained the face-to-face teaching contact with the children.

It took him a moment to meet her eyes. He already knew all he needed to about this woman without reading her CV. 'And the job situation is so bad that you were forced to consider relocating to the other end of the country?'

'So only rejects need apply, is that what you're saying?' she snipped back.

His moulded lips tightened. 'I'm saying that a woman like you would not last ten minutes here before she got bored, and the children here deserve continuity.' He stopped, realising that anyone listening might consider he felt the need to defend his position. His jaw tightened. He didn't.

Her chin went up. 'Mr Urquart, you know nothing about a woman like me.'

He huffed a cynical laugh. 'You'd be surprised.'

Anna threw up her hands, unable to control her exasperation. 'It really doesn't matter what I say, does it? You'll never give me a fair hearing because you've already made up your mind,' she accused.

His nostrils flared at the accusation. Ignoring the voice in the back of his head that suggested he might not be applying the objectivity he was famed for to this situation, he retorted coldly, 'My personal feelings have nothing whatever to do with this.'

Anna gave a disbelieving snort and chimed with bitter mockery, 'Lucky you.'

Cesare did not deign to respond. 'My sister is her own woman.'

Wishing her top were thicker, Anna folded her arms across her chest and masked her growing inability to hide her physical reaction to his aura of animal magnetism that lurked behind an expression of amused indifference.

How was it possible to loathe a man and still find yourself a helpless victim of his earthy sexuality? Why deny it? Her time and energy were better spent fighting it...him, herself.

'You make it sound like that's a bad thing.' Taking a breath to slow the agitated flow of words, she managed a condescending sniff. 'But then, I suppose for you it is.'

It was obvious to Anna that he wasn't the sort of man who would consider a mind of her own a good thing in a woman. It was easy to imagine the sort of female he liked, the variety who pandered to his vanity and acted as if every syllable he uttered were pure gold, just because he was famous and rich.

She sniffed. All right, there were probably other reasons too. She had to concede that even had Cesare Urquart been destitute and wearing rags there would still be plenty of women willing to overlook his flaws, willing to put up with a lot to be given access to that gorgeous...hard...male body.

Huffing out a tiny shocked gasp, she forced her eyes back to his face as she reminded herself that she was not—definitely not—one of those women. She preferred her men grounded and safe. Men like her ex, Mark.

Not that that relationship had been a great success!

Taking lust and hormones out of the equation had not saved Anna from making a mistake, but on the plus side that mistake had not involved an unplanned pregnancy, or a suicide attempt. Far better to be dumped by a man you didn't love, than one you couldn't live without.

She squeezed her eyes shut. She would never allow herself to be the victim that Rosie had, never allow a man to reduce her to that!

'My sister appears to trust you.'

Her tightly squeezed eyes opened and settled on his lean dark face before narrowing on the strong, sensual outline of his lips. Anna felt her stomach muscles tighten. Face it, taking lust and hormones out of the equation was not an option with a man who possessed that mouth!

'If you fail to live up to her expectations you will regret it.'

For several moments Anna remained too shocked by her own thought processes to respond.

'Is that a threat, Mr Urquart?' she finally asked quietly.

His dark eyebrows rose upwards. 'It is a fact, Miss Henderson,' he responded, without missing a beat.

Anna's chin lifted, her blue eyes narrowed at the corners, darkening with purpose as she met his stare head-on. Excitement was not a sane response to the warning, yet it was there in the shiver that slid like a silken finger down her spine.

Neither willing to be the first to break that contact, it was Cesare who did so, his glance sliding down the smooth column of her throat. The action bearing all the hallmarks of a compulsion that glittered in his heavy-lidded eyes as they reached the base of her throat where a pulse visibly pounded against her blue-veined skin. Skin that had a translucent sheen. It looked so soft that before he could exert some control he was visualising his open mouth pressed to that pulse spot while he slid his hand over the full provocative curve of her breast. He inhaled sharply, his expression hardening as he snarled, 'I do not tolerate incompetence in my staff.'

Anna's chin lifted another notch. It was not his arrogant assertion that sent her stomach into a dipping dive or brought a sheen of sweat to her skin, but the gleam she had seen in his deep-set eyes, a gleam that was sizzlingly hot as his voice was now cold.

'I'm not your staff.' She gave a haughty toss of her head. 'Now if you'd direct me I can get the things I left in the car and start doing what I came here for.'

It was not his words that finally made her pull in a tense breath and blank her expression but her reaction—the rush of excitement she experienced—when he said in a voice like cold steel, 'You are in my home. The rules are mine.'

He walked straight past her without having directed her anywhere. It was several minutes before Anna moved, before her shaking legs would support her. She had always firmly believed that the entire macho thing masked insecurity and had been mildly contemptuous of women who fell for the chest-beating routine.

But if Cesare had any insecurities he was hiding them well!

CHAPTER FIVE

ON HER SECOND day at Killaran, having dropped Jas off at her friend Samantha's house, Anna found she had a few hours to herself. She spent them exploring a section of the coastal path that would have been too taxing for Jasmine to cope with, though it was hard to convince the child she had any limitations.

By the time Anna had completed the coastal circuit and Killaran was in view, the exertion had unknotted some of the tension that had built up in her shoulders and brought a healthy flush to her cheeks. She tried not to let the sight of the grey stone monument that dominated the landscape spoil her mood. It was not the building that caused the spring in her step to grow heavy, it was the owner—Mr 'Lord of all I survey' Urquart.

At least he wouldn't be there to appear when she wasn't expecting it. Yesterday she had felt as though she were taking part in some sort of covert military exercise and she wasn't discounting the possibility her room had been bugged. Everywhere she went he was there, though what sinful activity he expected to catch her out in she didn't have a clue. Her relief had been so intense she nearly kissed the stern Mrs Mack when the housekeeper had explained that Monday mornings Cesare flew to Rome, returning in the middle of the week.

A few days a week without him around might just make this bearable. She hadn't been expecting him to back down, but she had thought he would accept the situation and let her get on with it, contenting himself with throwing the occasional scowl her way when their paths crossed occasionally. But if yesterday was any indicator she'd been wrong on both counts; this was a war of attrition.

And she couldn't do a damned thing about it. Jas was his niece. She could hardly restrict his access and the child clearly adored him. Having decided he had no redeeming features, she found it very annoying to have him turn out to be child friendly.

But she wouldn't let him grind her down, it was obvious to Anna that where Cesare Urquart was concerned everything had to be his way or not at all. The man simply couldn't tolerate not being the one calling the shots; he had to be in charge and flex his macho muscles. Well, not with me, she thought defiantly.

She knew he was looking for an excuse to get rid of her and she was equally determined not to give it. Pushing the thoughts of the absent castle owner out of her head, she glanced at her watch and discovered she had an entire hour to spare before she needed to collect Jas.

Remembering the book she had downloaded to read on the journey up, she entered the castle through the side entrance, then paused now she almost had her bearings. The place was a total maze but she knew that the most direct route to the apartment was through the front door and down an inner connecting corridor.

If there had been any chance of bumping into the man who had appointed himself her judge, jury and, if she gave him the chance, executioner, there was no way in the world she would have taken that route, but today she would be safe.

The connecting door lay at the end of a long stone-floored corridor. There were a dozen doors that opened off it on either side and the walls were lined with framed antique political prints. She resisted the temptation to study them, speeding up as she walked past the one open door, catching a glimpse of boo-lined walls and the glow of a log fire reflected in an enormous mirror.

She had gone a dozen steps when she stopped, unable to resist taking a second look. She backtracked. There was something about a book. Although she loved the convenience of the novel waiting on her tablet, it lacked the sheer tactile experience of holding a book.

As she poked her head around the door she let out a silent whistle and stepped inside. The room was not as big as the baronial hall, nor as impressive as the ball-room with the intricately moulded hand-painted ceiling and tapestry-lined walls, but this room had something, a lived-in warmth that drew her.

She inhaled deeply and sighed. 'It probably makes me insane but I just love the smell of books!'

'There are worse smells.' Like the light fragrance she favoured, delicate but somehow he had smelt it as she hurried past the door; it was stronger now she was inside the room.

Anna's head snapped sideways in time for her to see Cesare rise with lazy fluid grace from a high-backed chair facing the window. She watched as he straightened to his full impressive height. Long and lean, every inch of him hard. She swallowed and felt something kick hard in her stomach. The sensation spread, rippling out across her skin until her flesh was hot yet pebbled in goosebumps.

'You're not here.'

He raised a sardonic brow.

The colour that had drained from her face rushed back with a vengeance. 'I mean, I thought you were away or I wouldn't have...'

'Got caught.'

'I'm sorry if I intruded,' she said stiffly, 'but this is a lovely room.'

She bit down on her lip. If she started to babble nervously she might not be able to stop. Was it possible to talk yourself to death? That such a thing as death by metallic stare existed was a lot less uncertain!

'I think so.'

Another nerve-shredding silence fell and still his silvered stare held her in a grip that made her feel like a butterfly on a pin. It was easy to visualise barbaric images around this man. It was even easier to think about his hard muscles and smooth skin.

She scrunched her eyes shut and blinked in an effort to banish the relentless reel of erotic images playing in her head. When she opened them he was no longer looking at her. She took a small sideways step as the downgraded tension level made her knees give.

'This is where I work when I'm home.' Not that he had been working. The tension humming in his veins had made concentration impossible.

Finally freed of the surgical-steel stare, Anna began to look around the room. Anywhere but at him. She saw no visible evidence of work but resisted the childish temptation to mention this; instead she took a deep breath. It might hurt but, like it or not, on this occasion she was in the wrong.

'I'm sorry if I disturbed you,' Then, aware that her stiff delivery sounded unconvincing, added, 'Really.'

Her wary eyes trained on his face. There was a limit to how long you could stare over someone's shoulder without causing comment. She saw a muscle clench in his cheek and wondered why she'd bothered to do the right thing when all her apology had done was make him look murderously angry. She might have assumed that was the norm for him if she hadn't seen him with his niece. The Cesare she saw with Jas was hardly recognisable as this sneering, autocratic monster.

She took a step towards the door. 'I'll leave you in peace.'

Peace!

Cesare wiped the back of his hand across his mouth and felt the moisture along his upper lip. Another couple of seconds and he would have convinced himself that a taste of her lips would be enough; the next step would have been deciding that he could handle sex with her. He was not sure why he wanted her so much beyond the obvious, but he was sure that he would not have any peace until he had ejected this woman from his home, his life and his head.

It would have been easier if Jas hadn't so obviously taken to her, but like her impulsive mother the little girl had taken one look at Anna Henderson and decided she was a kindred spirit.

Unable to fight the impulse, he lowered his gaze to her lips. Again in his head he could see them swollen from his kisses. Contemptuous of his own lack of control, he pushed the image away. It wasn't her occupation of his head he had to worry about. His head had very little to do with what was happening. Something about her bypassed his intellect—his reaction to her was all about blind instinct and simple lust.

'Where is my niece?'

Framed in the doorway, Anna turned back to face the accusation, the action causing her hair to whip around her face. 'She's playing with a friend.' She brushed back the fiery strands from her cheek, hating the defensive note she could hear in her voice.

'So the first chance you get you offload your responsibilities to someone else?'

On the scale of the unfairness he had displayed so far this accusation rated fairly low, but it was just one hit too many. Something inside her snapped. She gritted her teeth and glared at him in utter frustration. She didn't expect life to be fair but this was ridiculous.

'Jas is playing with a friend. I haven't locked her in her bedroom and gone out shopping or worse.' She shook her head and threw up her hands in a gesture of angry frustration, then, about to turn away, changed her mind and took two angry steps in his direction.

Her chest lifting in tune with her angry agitated breathing, she stood, hands on her hips, her chin thrust out, and she glared up at him while covering her upper lip with her plump lower one to huff stray wisps of hair from her face. 'Why are you here today anyway?' She wiped a persistent strand of hair that was tickling her nose, 'Could it be you wanted to be around so you could stalk me again?'

He sucked in an outraged breath and dragged his eyes off her mouth. 'Stalk?'

There was danger in his echo that sent a shiver down Anna's spine. Problem was the shiver was not trepidation, it was anticipation. She needed to end the conversation and get out of here very quickly.

You should always finish something you started.

There was only one place this was going to finish. The electricity in the air was humming, the sexual tension off the scale.

'I don't stalk women.'

She struggled to escape his smoky stare. 'You know what I mean.'

'Though a few have been known to stalk me.'

She wrinkled her nose in distaste; she'd just bet they had.

'I'm happy for you,' she lied. 'You've already made sure I didn't get the job. Isn't that enough for you? Or do you have to continue this...this p-persecution?'

'I told you how it would be, so don't turn on the injured act.' Did she know how sexy that damned stutter was?

Of course she did.

Anna responded to his cold delivery with an extra spurt of temper. 'I remember! Your house, your rules. I get it, I really do, and I know you're waiting for me to mess up, but what I don't get is what do you think I'm going to do? Invite all the married men from a ten-mile radius to an orgy on the lawn with Jasmine watching?'

He ground out a word in Italian that stopped her mid-flow. She went still, her eyes widening as she bit down hard on her full lower lip. She could have kicked herself for rising to the bait.

His eyes, as he stared down at her, reminded Anna of smoked glass. She couldn't even see herself, let alone what he was thinking, but lines of tension that radiated from the corners of his mouth and the audible sound of the deep breaths he was taking suggested that under the mask he was as mad as hell.

'It's not very pleasant feeling as if I'm on trial, being watched,' she muttered, looking up at him through her lashes, not backing down but stopping short of a head-on collision.

His response was immediate, his solution simple. 'If you don't like it, then there's a solution—pack your bags and leave.'

'My God, is this an example of that famous Highland hospitality, or is this Italian warmth?'

She watched his beautiful mouth tighten but instead of responding he adopted an attitude of silent superiority that had a red-rag effect on Anna.

In a calmer state of mind she would have known it was a dangerous road to go down, but she wasn't calm. She was so angry she delivered the first, smartest, though not most sensible, thing that came into her head and challenged scornfully, 'What's your problem? Do I scare you or something?'

It didn't even cross her mind that she might hit a nerve, or more likely his planet-sized ego, until his head reared back as though she had struck him.

He didn't speak, he just reached out; he must have moved but she wasn't conscious of it. Just of him touching the side of her face, his hand cupped over her cheek, just one finger actually in contact with her skin. The gentle whisper of movement a stark contrast to the violence of the emotions that shimmered in the electrically charged air.

She heard a noise but didn't actually connect it to her gasp. Her eyes were closed, her chest was so tight that she stopped breathing as she struggled and failed to stop herself turning her face into his palm like a flower seeking sun. The feelings that churned in her belly were not light, they were dark and hot.

Then, just as her knees were giving, he pushed her away.

Anna took a staggering step back. He had taken two and he was standing feet away, not up close where she could feel the heat of his skin through her clothes. She suddenly shivered.

'What was that meant to prove?'

He dragged a not quite steady hand down his jaw. Prove? Did she actually think he had put some thought into his actions? That he was following some logical process: press button A and...? The problem was she was pressing all his buttons and acting as if she didn't know it.

The knowledge that he was acting like all those poor dumb losers he'd watched while he was growing up didn't sit well with him. Those too were intelligent men who made fools of themselves over his mother. For her part, she was never intentionally cruel; she just saw what she wanted and went for it.

'What the heart wants, Cesare...'

He could hear her now, see her little shrug in response to any hint of criticism. 'What the heart wants, Cesare...'

His mother's heart had been disastrously drawn to married men and it had remained miraculously unaffected when she walked away from her affairs. The same could not have been said for the men who fell for her. Cesare had always wondered if had just one time the tables been reversed, and she had been the one given a glimpse of paradise then dumped in the cold, she might have cleaned up her act.

It never happened.

And this woman was the same. But he wasn't a victim. Not like his friend, Paul, who had nearly abandoned his wife for her.

Neither was he married. He was a free agent, and his heart was definitely not involved. He was, it might be argued, exactly the sort of man who might one day give this tempting little witch a taste of her own medicine. A man who stood in no danger of being sucked in by the sexy catch in her husky voice or the innocent hurt in those big blue eyes.

It was not an argument he was about to make. He wanted to keep the hell away from her. He wanted her out of his life.

The big blue eyes in question were at that moment angry, not hurt, as they connected with his. 'I know you think I'm some sort of home wrecker...' she stated, unwittingly tuning into his train of thought.

'But actually I'm not.' She stopped and thought, What am I doing? I don't give a damn what he thinks of me...I don't owe him any explanations. Better he think I'm a slut than Rosie, who isn't here to defend herself. 'That desperate.'

'Desperate?'

'Well, the only person around here that I could have my evil way with is you.' She gave a laugh and waited but there was nothing, not even a flicker in his face.

The spark of uncertainty that moved at the back of her eyes morphed into something close to panic. He couldn't have interpreted the comment as a proposition?

Mouth dry, she swallowed hard—could he?

'And that isn't, I promise you, going to happen.'

Her hasty husky addendum drew a smile that belonged to a predator at the top of the food chain. The butterfly kicks in her stomach became wild somersaults as Anna lifted her chin and tried not to act like a trapped furry creature.

'Because you find me so physically repulsive?' he suggested, with the silky confidence of a man who had never been knocked back in his life. More was the pity—it might have made him more human.

In that moment she really hated him. 'It's not all about looks.'

And now she got her laugh—not a nice one. It made Anna, the most pacifist of people, want quite badly to kill him.

'Of course not! A sensible woman like you would not latch onto a man who doesn't have the money to lavish her with life's little luxuries.'

She wanted to respond to the nasty irony with a shrug, and had his insults been aimed at her Anna might have been able to, but, although he didn't realise it, it was her cousin he was insulting. Anna knew it was Rosie that he was as good as calling some sort of call girl and it was this that made it impossible for Anna to bite her tongue. As if he were in any position to make moral judgements, she fumed. You only had to type his name into a laptop and the information that coughed up made it clear that his sister had not exaggerated when she had accused him of being a serial seducer!

He arched a satiric brow, his smile morphing into a frown as he watched the flush travel up her neck until her face was burning. She blushed like some little outraged virgin! Part, presumably, of her charm?

His expressive mouth twisted into a grimace of scornful distaste. If some men found inexperience, the thought of teaching a novice the ropes, a turn-on, he was not one of them! If virgins had been a traffic problem he would have made a detour. He was attracted to women as open-minded and as sexually experienced as he was, women who did not come with emotional baggage or make any demands. There was not, in his experience, a shortage of such women.

His pleated brow smoothed. The mistake with Anna Henderson would be to be taken in by appearances. This woman was as experienced sexually as any of his partners, just not as upfront about it. Cesare, who admired straight talking and honesty, found her artifice contemptible. Unfortunately his contempt stopped short of preventing him from wanting to rip off her clothes, and his own, while kissing those lying, delicious lips and finding out if they lived up to the tempting promise of the lush fullness. He knew they would, and he also knew that the moment he touched her there would be no going back.

That was one genie he intended to leave safely locked in its bottle.

'I'm sure you've been told this many times before, but your modesty is one of the most endearing things about you.' Anna bit out the sarcastic jibe through clenched white teeth. 'I hate to break it to you but I think I could do better than a has-been racing driver with megalomaniac tendencies. You're not bad-looking but you're not nearly as irresistible as you think you are.'

By the time she had reached her breathless conclusion his eyebrows had hit his ebony hairline. Well, tough, she thought, clinging tenaciously to her defiance. If he could dish it out, he ought to be prepared to take it. Rosie wasn't here to defend herself, but Anna was and she was going to.

She had taken an almost indecent delight in shredding him. His eyes dropped to her mouth. He would take an equal amount of delight in making her eat her words. The contemplation of that pleasure elevated the ache in his groin to another painful level.

Laughter was not a reaction she had anticipated but before she could even think about reacting to the low throaty growl, he stepped into her and, holding her eyes with his gaze, he grabbed her waist, looping one arm right around her middle and hauling her hard up against him. The action effortless, almost casual. Warmth flooded through her at his touch, then he brought his mouth down hard on her lips.

Not casual, and the heat became fire.

It was not a gentle kiss, no coaxing tenderness, just hungry demand, nothing equal in it. This was about exerting control. It did not start slow and build up, it just exploded. Before Anna closed her eyes the whimper in her throat was lost in his mouth. She saw the flames in his eyes so hot that her insides melted.

She struggled to rise above it. So he knew his way around a kiss. So what? It was only to be expected. Just a kiss, but his warm, musky male scent was filling her nostrils, the heat of his lean body was seeping into her bones, the impression of the arousal he did not attempt to disguise was grinding into the vulnerable softness of her pelvis. After the first shocked gasp she moved against him, squirming to increase the erotic pressure. The dull pounding in her head felt like a drum beat as she freed her trapped hands from between their bodies and linked her hands around his neck, giving a throaty murmur as she opened her mouth to the pressure of his probing tongue's silken hot invasion.

Conflict would come later. Now she gave herself up, allowed herself to be consumed. She wanted it, she was flame and fire, not earthbound. Her head was spinning, her legs did not belong to her, her heart was pounding, the dark blood thrumming in every part of her.

Not just a kiss, never just a kiss! This was a master class in seduction. Having lost control of her body, Anna struggled to retain control of her mind and in one small corner managed to distance herself from what was happening.

His lips finally lifted just a fraction, leaving a whisper of air between them. The seal broken, his thumb remained under her jaw. She didn't remember how it got there. He was still close enough for her to feel his warm breath on her mouth, but far enough away for her to claw her way out of the sensual fog that had enveloped her.

Reality hit her with the force of icy water. Panting she pressed her hands flat against the iron-hard barrier of his chest and pushed. The force behind the push was pretty feeble; he, on the other hand, was not. He was all hard muscle and bone so when he reacted and released her, caught unawares, Anna staggered back several steps before she regained her centre of gravity.

It was a toss-up who he was most furious with: her for goading him, or himself for reacting.

If he had ever wondered why Paul had made a total fool of himself, he now knew. He had always believed there was some truth in the old adage about knowledge and power, but in this case peace of mind did not go hand in hand with that supposed power.

'Get the hell out of here!' he flung.

Anna managed a glare of sorts but continued to shake. Regardless of the image she might present, she was glued to the spot, her stomach churning with a toxic mixture of shame, self-loathing and shock.

She took refuge in a technicality and lifted her chin to an imperious angle. 'You can't sack me—you don't pay my salary.'

'I wasn't sacking you, I was telling...' he arched a sardonic brow '...sorry, requesting, you to get out of my sight unless you fancy a repeat.'

The power returned to Anna's legs and she fled. Not the dignified option but definitely the most sensible!

CHAPTER SIX

THE NEXT DAY Anna spent the morning studiously avoiding any place where she might bump into Cesare. She sensed his presence around every corner and had begun to jump at her own shadow to the point where Jas had asked if she was all right.

This from a five-year-old!

It was a wake-up call. What the hell was she doing creeping around as though she had something to feel guilty for? He was the one who had kissed her—admittedly, technically speaking, she had kissed him back. She had fallen into that kiss with an uninhibited enthusiasm that she hadn't known she was capable of.

Forget the kiss and move on. A good idea but there was no escaping the inescapable—moving on involved seeing this man again at some point. She had to be positive and take the initiative. She'd choose her battle site, do it on her terms.

It was ironic that when she had decided to confront him she discovered that he wasn't even there.

Cesare had flown out to Rome early that morning.

And good riddance!

There was a strong element of anticlimax mixed in

with her relief. Though she threw herself into doing what she was being paid for—caring for Jasmine. It wasn't a chore, more a life line.

Seeing the world through a child's eyes was something that never palled. It was the reason that she had loved teaching, and Jas was a particularly delightful child.

Anna was prevented from enjoying the next couple of days by the knowledge that he would be back, that this reprieve was only temporary.

On the Friday Cesare returned to Killaran, but he wasn't alone.

Anna, out on a walk with Jasmine at the time, didn't see the woman who got out of the helicopter with him, but the news was around the castle in a matter of seconds. Before they had walked through the baronial entrance hall, all the staff knew she was a blonde, beautiful, thirty something, a divorced, successful corporate lawyer. Her name was Louise Gove.

Anna hadn't even got her coat off before she received all the details from the group gathered around the kitchen table to discuss the momentous event. She didn't question how they knew all this, nor did she question or even acknowledge her gut-churning reaction to this information.

Keeping her voice low so her comment didn't reach Jasmine, who, still in her boots and coat, had followed her nose and the doting cook to the walk-in larder where by tradition she got to take her pick of the newly baked cakes cooling on the big slate shelf, Anna posed the obvious question.

'This can't be the first time that he's brought a girl-friend home?' Especially considering the very high turnover, she thought bitterly.

It turned out she was wrong.

It seemed that although he frequently entertained at the castle—the staff was proud of the lavish occasions they catered and the important guests from film stars to diplomats they looked after—Cesare never brought his lover of the moment to Killaran.

'So it stands to reason this one must be special.'

The only questions as far as anyone was concerned appeared to be when the wedding would be, would there be any changes and did she deserve him?

'What do you think, Anna?'

'I think she deserves our pity!' Her heartfelt out-burst earned her a few startled and openly speculative looks, because weirdly the staff here were rather pro-tective of their boss.

Anna lifted her shoulders in a shrug. 'What? Do you really believe a sexual predator undergoes a personal-ity change just because he gets married?'

Before any of the staff had a chance to respond to her comment a small voice interrupted.

'What's a sex...usual predate?'

A guilty flush rose to Anna's cheeks as she turned and saw the little girl holding a cupcake in one hand.

'Were you talking about Uncle Cesare?' Her green eyes lit up. 'Is he back home?'

Home was traditionally where the heart was. Had Cesare brought his heart with him in the shape of a beautiful blonde? 'I think he just arrived, sweetheart.'

With an excited whoop his niece was out of the room before Anna could stop her impetuous dash. In her haste to follow, Anna knocked over a mug of coffee on the table. The delay meant the little girl had reached the library door before Anna caught up with her.

'No, Jas, your uncle might be too busy.' He might be too occupied, she thought, and felt queasy as an image of Cesare with the tall, beautiful, blonde possible future bride in his arms flashed into her head.

'He won't be too busy for me,' the little girl declared confidently before she pushed open the door.

Even before they had stepped out of the helicopter Cesare was regretting his spur-of-the-moment decision to extend the invitation to Louise. Not that he had a problem with Louise herself, he just preferred to keep the compartments of his life separate and, though his sister had never commented, he knew she appreciated that he did not parade his lovers in front of her impressionable daughter.

They both had personal experience of what it was like to grow fond of someone who simply vanished one day—though sometimes he and Angel had been only too glad to see them disappear.

'Uncles' grew less of a problem for Cesare after his growth spurt when he was sixteen. Almost overnight he turned from a gangly teen into a muscular six feet plus. For Angel the problems got worse when she grew and Cesare, away at university, had not been around to protect her. His expression grew sombre as he recalled the scene he had walked in on, his fourteen-year-old sister fighting off a slobbering 'uncle', who had waved a branch of mistletoe when he saw Cesare.

The 'uncle' had spent that Christmas nursing a broken jaw in hospital, and he and Angel had spent it in a hotel. After that Angel had spent weekends with him and mid-week boarding.

He pushed away the memories—Cesare preferred to live in the present—along with his misgivings. It was only a weekend, he was hardly inviting Louise to take up residence. He seriously doubted that the successful litigator with whom he had enjoyed a short and pleasant association the year before would feel inclined to get her clothes grubby playing with a child.

When Louise had wafted fragrantly into a meeting as the legal representative of a rival company Cesare had found himself sitting opposite the perfect solution to the classic signs of sexual frustration he had been exhibiting.

After the meeting it had been Louise who had approached him. Was he involved? she had asked, making it clear once he had said he wasn't that she would not be averse to rekindling the affair.

The only setback had been the business dinner she needed to attend in Paris that evening, but she would, she had assured him, be available the next day. She was flying back to London bright and early and had the whole weekend free.

'I have to be in Scotland this weekend.' Normally he would have been able to shrug off this case of bad timing but instead he heard himself saying, 'Why don't you join me?'

Once the offer was made and accepted he could not withdraw it and why would he want to? A weekend with the lovely Louise in his bed would be a perfect cure for the redhead who was in danger of becoming an obsession with him. There had been no sign of her when he landed, not that he had been looking for her specifically but Jas usually ran to greet him and claim the token present he always brought her when he returned.

'You have a lovely home. I hope you have these insured?' She ran her finger down a leather spine.

Cesare dragged his attention back to his beautiful companion who was examining a row of first editions on the shelf just as the door was flung open.

'Sorry.' Anna, following close behind the excited child, bent forward to grab her charge but missed as Jasmine pushed excitedly by her and straight at Cesare's outstretched hand.

'What have you got me?'

'Who says I've got you anything, kiddo?' While he bent to angle a teasing look at his diminutive niece, in the periphery of his vision he was aware of another figure. He straightened up and watched Jas tear the paper off the gift she had extracted from his pocket before he turned his gaze her way.

Louise's presence did not protect him from the streak of white-hot lust that shot through his body. With the lust came the reluctant acknowledgement that the explanation for the impulse behind the uncharacteristic invitation to the beautiful lawyer had little to do with the pleasure of her company or even the prospect of steamy sex. He had wanted to demonstrate to Anna

Henderson that there were men who could kiss her and walk away without a backward glance. He could see now that the need to prove something, even to himself, was in itself a weakness. Wanting to catch a glimpse of jealousy on Anna Henderson's face... That was hardly a sign of indifference.

He expelled a long slow breath and found his gaze drawn irresistibly to the face in question. His eyes roamed the delicate contours, the softly flushed cheeks, the small nose sprinkled with freckles and the mouth smiling now as she looked at Jasmine. A mouth that promised sensual delight and delivered on that promise.

Not allowing himself the dangerous indulgence, he pushed away the memory before it had fully surfaced and exhaled in a series of carefully controlled breaths. This was all about control and exerting it, all about not being a victim of his own hormones or the lush promise of her lips.

As if feeling his eyes, she turned her head. As their glances connected he saw wariness in those blue iridescent pools and also a need that made the ache in his groin tighten another painful notch.

He thought of Paul. It should have been enough to quench the hunger—it wasn't.

'Uncle Cesare, we lifted a stone and counted the different creepy-crawly things underneath. They were totally gross! You'll never in a billion years guess how many there were. Uncle Cesare?'

Dark lines scoring the chiselled angles of his cheekbones, Cesare wrenched his stare free of those blue eyes and responded to the sharp imperative tug on his sleeve.

'Were you listening?'

He cleared his throat before answering the charge. 'A billion?'

'No, stupid, twenty-two.'

His dark smouldering stare had deconstructed Anna's careful rationalisation of that kiss and her shameful response brick by brick. She had never wanted to know what real passion felt like, the sort that made otherwise sensible women like Rosie act foolishly for men who were so obviously no good for them. She still believed there was always a choice, but now she understood why some women made the wrong choice.

She wouldn't, but still... Heart pumping like an overstretched piston, she watched him grin. It softened the lines of tension from his handsome face, managing in the process to make him look even more wildly attractive and years younger.

She felt the dangerous weakening of her antagonism and reminded herself that even monsters had soft spots. Some loved their mother or their dog, and maybe this monster loved a tall blonde with the sort of grooming she would never achieve?

Jaw clenched, she slid a surreptitious look at the other woman. Tall and elegant in a silk shirt and high-waisted, wide-legged linen trousers that emphasised her endless legs and tiny waist. The woman with her sleek bobbed hair, immaculate appearance and perfect figure made Anna feel hopelessly inadequate, but on the plus side having her around might mean Cesare wouldn't have the time to be on her case so much.

The thought of him being too exhausted after a night

of relentless steamy passion with the ice queen here afforded Anna surprisingly little comfort, though it was hard to imagine that hair mussed.

Not so hard to imagine those long crimson-tipped fingers running over his golden skin. She recalled the feel of the hair-roughened skin of his face and flexed her tingling fingertips before she smothered the memory under several layers of antagonism and stubborn resolve. If he still continued to harass her even with his girlfriend around she would rise above it and simply ignore him. Anticipating her occupation of the moral high ground, she lifted her chin.

'Look what I've got, Anna.'

Anna gave herself a mental shake and dutifully examined the tiny house, perfect in every detail, beautifully carved out of wood. She turned it over in her hand before handing the beautifully crafted piece back to Jasmine.

'You have quite a collection now.' Jasmine had confided her intention of building an entire village with the pieces her uncle brought her back from his trips.

'Nearly a complete street now and the church. Thank you, Uncle Cesare.'

He tipped his dark head in acknowledgement. 'You are welcome.' He laid a hand on Louise's arm. 'My niece, Jasmine. Say hello to Miss Gove, Jas.'

'Hello.'

'I had no idea you had a niece. Why, isn't she a darling? Call me Auntie Louise.'

'Why? You're not my auntie.'

The tall blonde bent down towards Jas but jerked

back in alarm at the last moment. 'Goodness, you're covered in mud!'

'So is Anna,' Jas offered by way of defence.

'But I don't have frosting all around my mouth,' Anna retorted, pulling a tissue from her pocket to wipe around Jas's cupid-bow lips.

As the comment drew the tall, elegant couple's attention Anna stood there and endured the scrutiny, feeling her cheeks heat. It was hard to see what was going on behind his smoked-glass stare but the woman looked amused.

'Goodness, so she is.' Her wrinkled nose, as much as her pristine white shift dress, made Anna conscious of the contrast she must make. 'You're the nanny?'

Not quite sure how to respond, Anna found herself glancing Cesare's way.

'Miss Henderson is helping Angel out for a few weeks as a sort of glorified babysitter.'

Jas tugged her uncle's sleeve. 'Call her Anna. She's not my teacher.' She giggled as if the idea was hilarious.

It was the tall blonde with her scarlet claws on Cesare's arm who broke the pregnant silence.

'I admire teachers,' she said unexpectedly. 'Not a job I could do, though,' she admitted, instantly going up in Anna's estimation. 'I'm sure your job has a lot of satisfaction too and without all that responsibility.'

Anna produced a fake smile and realised that first impressions were normally spot on. 'Now there's a thought,' she drawled, directing her stare straight at Cesare, who returned it without any visible sign of discomfiture.

'Children are the future.'

Anna just managed not to roll her eyes while his companion acted as though he'd just voiced something profound, not blindingly obvious. 'How true,' Louise said earnestly.

'I think that the people who care for them should be above reproach, don't you, Miss Henderson?'

Anna, who chose to ignore the dig, lifted her chin. 'Don't ask me, I'm in it for the money, status and prestige. Come along, Jas, we need to clean up.' Before she took the child's hand Anna thought she caught a flash of something approaching amusement in his slate-coloured eyes, but, no, it must have been a trick of the light. He didn't possess a sense of humour...just a great body and formidable sex appeal.

It didn't matter how many times he knocked her down verbally, Cesare mused, Anna always got up, brushed herself off and came out fighting. He had waited for her to put a foot wrong, but she hadn't. His initial concerns for his niece's welfare in Anna's charge had diminished. It was now his welfare that concerned him—her presence was driving him insane.

'Looks like I'm in the wrong job,' Louise drawled, watching the two make their way across the cobbled courtyard. 'I think I offended your nanny,' she teased lightly.

'She's not my nanny,' he gritted back, his eyes still trained on the retreating flame-haired figure. Her walk was like the woman herself—provocative! The swing of her hips, the way she... He clenched his jaw and refused to acknowledge the lustful surge of hunger in his blood and snarled, 'She's a damned pain in the—' He caught Louise's startled expression and forced a smile while he dragged a hand down his jaw. 'She is Angel's choice, not mine.'

'So get rid of her.'

'There's nothing I'd like more.' A life without those blue eyes judging him. A house without that husky laugh or the perfume that lingered in rooms.

He knew there was a simple solution to his problem. They might be living under the same roof but that roof did not cover a two-up two-down cottage. It would have been easy to avoid the rooms where her scent might linger, remain safely out of hearing distance of her aggravating laugh.

But that would mean putting his own comfort ahead of Jasmine's well-being. He needed to stay vigilant; he had to be there to step in if needed. This was not about his personal comfort.

Noble Cesare, mocked the voice in his head.

'I've never seen you like this,' Louise decided, studying his face. 'I can look at her contract if that's the problem?'

'I doubt very much she has one.'

Louise looked shocked by the admission. 'Then legally—'

Cesare took a deep breath. 'I appreciate the offer, Louise, but I have it under control.' If only.

Louise suddenly let out a startled laugh. 'It's her, isn't it? The nanny. There's something going on between you two.'

'Of course there isn't something going on.'

But Louise had her litigator's hat on and she wasn't letting go. 'I wondered why you invited me here, but you wanted to make this girl jealous, didn't you?' She released a husky laugh.

Cesare scowled. 'Don't be ridiculous!'

'Well, well. For once in your life you're doing the running, aren't you, Cesare?'

CHAPTER SEVEN

LEAVING JAS SITTING in front of the computer screen chatting excitedly to her mother, Anna walked through to the adjoining room to take her call.

It was her aunt Jane with the news that Rosie had started getting pains the previous night. They had all gone to hospital but it had turned out to be a false alarm. Anna laughed when her aunt described the journey there, sent her sympathy to Rosie, who had lost sight of her feet, and wished she too could be there.

Anna, who had smiled all the way through the phone conversation, felt strangely flat after she put the phone down. She realised the heaviness in her chest was homesickness—not for a place but for her family. Rosie was not just her cousin, she was her best friend, and if she had been here Anna would have been at the birth and later she'd have been toasting the baby with the proud grandparents, who had decided to stay on an extra few weeks in Canada before they flew back home.

She took a deep breath, told herself not to be stupid—things didn't stay the same. Having Rosie safe and happy with her gorgeous husband, Scott, in another country was a lot better than an unhappy Rosie living within walking distance.

She would visit next Christmas as they'd planned and she'd be a doting aunt.

When she walked back into Jasmine's bedroom a few minutes later the little girl was blowing kisses at the screen.

'You go clean your teeth, there's a good girl, and Mummy will give you another story tomorrow.'

Watching Jasmine skip from the room, Anna bent down to see the computer screen, her smile fading as she saw the tears running down Angel's face.

'What's wrong?' she asked, slipping into the seat the child had just vacated.

Angel shook her head and gave a sniff before wiping the moisture from her face. 'I miss her so much. I just wish…' She gave a sigh and produced a tremulous smile that just about broke Anna's heart. 'Ignore me, I'm just having a bad day—you know, sunshine, sand, palm trees.' She shook her head gave a wry grimace and drawled ironically, 'It's a tough life. You have no idea how exhausting it is to be forced to live in the lap of luxury in a five-star hotel and then to top it all be asked to wear beautiful clothes and have your face painted by experts.'

Anna was not fooled by the self-mocking grin. She knew that Angel would have given every glamorous trapping of her life to be able to hold her daughter on her lap while she read the bedtime story.

'So ignore me, how are you and is that big bad brother of mine behaving himself?'

Anna hadn't intended mentioning the house guest but she found herself blurting, 'He's brought a woman home.'

Angel's jaw dropped. 'Now that I didn't see coming. So what's she like?'

Anna struggled to be scrupulously fair in her assessment, though Angel's verdict of, 'She sounds terrible,' suggested she might not have succeeded.

Anna glanced at the illuminated clock on her bedside table, and groaned as she read the time. Three a.m. It had been two before she had finally dropped off.

She had lifted her pillow, intending to cover her head with it, when a muffled cry made her sit up straight, her head tilted to one side in an alert listening attitude, almost immediately the cry...no, sob...came again.

Anna was out of her bed in one leap, fired by urgency. She hit the floor running, fighting her way into her robe as she dashed down the corridor. Jasmine's room was two doors along. When she had looked in earlier the little girl had been fast asleep in the pretty canopied bed that was illuminated by a night light that cast shadows of birds on the wall above her head.

Jasmine was no longer asleep but sitting up in her bed, two patches of bright colour on her cheeks. The little girl's otherwise pale face was stained with tears.

'I was sick.'

'You poor thing.' Bending over the bed, Anna smoothed the damp curls from the little girl's feverish forehead and assessed the situation.

'I'm hot!'

'I know, darling, never mind—we'll have you sorted in two ticks,' Anna soothed.

It took a little longer than that. She sponged Jasmine and dressed her in a fresh pair of pyjamas, then sat the child, who was shivering even though her skin was hot, in an armchair while she changed the bed linen. 'Oh, you poor thing.'

Five minutes later Jas was back in her bed. Heavy-eyed, she looked on the point of falling back to sleep and not obviously distressed. In charge of a class of thirty six-year-olds for the past four years, Anna was not a stranger to childhood ailments, but the first call with unwell children had always been to contact the parents and clearly in this situation that was not possible.

With no Angel, second best would have to do.

Second best. She was willing to bet this term was not one that was generally applied to Cesare Urquart—the man had winner written all over him. Some people might find that attractive. Personally Anna found little to admire in men driven to prove they were the best at everything, the sort of men that people looked to for leadership. Well, she for one liked to make her own decisions, though in this instance she was glad this was not her call.

'I'm thirsty.'

Anna picked up the empty glass on the bedside table and went to the kitchen to fill it.

'Just sips,' she warned as she held it up to the fretful youngster's lips. 'Just wet your lips…better?'

Jasmine nodded and Anna kissed the little girl's forehead.

'I want Mummy.' The sniff and the trembling lip

completed a totally heartbreaking scene. If Angel had been able to see her daughter at that moment Anna had no doubt that contract or not, she would have been on the first plane home, and by then of course Jas would have forgotten she'd ever been ill!

'I know, sweetheart. How about if I fetch Uncle Cesare?'

Jasmine nodded. 'Yes, I want Uncle Cesare.'

Don't we all? chimed Anna's subconscious.

'I won't be long. You just snuggle down and I'll…' Drag your uncle from his warm bed. From his lover's arms. My, aren't I going to be the popular one? She breathed through a wave of nausea and wondered if she might have a dose of what afflicted Jasmine. 'Back in two ticks,' she promised.

When the housekeeper at Angel's request, had given her a tour on that first day, Anna had paid attention. She remembered Mrs Mack pointing out the staircase she now ran up, emphasising sternly it led to Mr Urquart's private quarters and was strictly off limits.

She had stopped short of saying so was the man himself, but the underlying message was clear. The poor woman obviously considered her boss a man irresistible to women and she had taken on the job of protecting him.

Somehow Anna had kept a straight face while being lectured on the strict hierarchy within the castle. A hierarchy that made it not the done thing to approach Cesare Urquart directly. There were channels, the housekeeper had informed her sternly.

Anna hadn't asked what the channels were. It was all

she could do to stop herself from informing the woman that approaching her precious boss was not something she was likely to be doing in a hurry.

Pity the woman hadn't told the man himself about the rules, though at three a.m., rules became a little blurred.

Jas's uncle would blame her. Fairness didn't come into it; reasonable was not in his vocabulary. He had been waiting for her to screw up and he'd probably be delighted to have a reason.

Not true, said the voice in her head, and you know it. Anna gave a reluctant sigh of acknowledgement. Whatever his faults, and he had many, not being protective or caring for his niece was not among them. There was no way he would have the child suffer to prove a point.

Poor little Jas. The thought of the girl made Anna almost philosophical about the blast of chilly contempt coming her way. He'd find some way of making this her fault, and maybe, she mused, he wasn't so wrong. She had noticed Jasmine's flushed cheeks at bedtime and instead of taking her temperature she'd put it down to the warm bath.

Angel might have said she was in charge, but she knew that in a situation like this she would not expect Anna to make a unilateral decision. The bottom line was she was just—what had he called her? A glorified babysitter. He'd meant it as an insult, but essentially it was an accurate description of her role.

It was Angel's brother who was the appropriate person to decide the correct course of action, and if ever a man was equipped to make decisions it was Jas's uncle.

It wasn't as if he'd waste time agonising over it. A

crooked smile briefly twisted her soft lips as an image
of the incumbent of the castle floated before her eyes.
Somehow she didn't think indecision was his style! Just
tall, snooty blondes with endless legs.

At the top of the spiral staircase there were doors
leading off a wide corridor. Four in total, but only one
had light coming from underneath it. There were sounds
of music, something bluesy, coming from behind the big
door and a tiny sliver of light shining under. The pucker
between her brows deepened. Did he not sleep? Or did
he suffer from insomnia? When the explanation came
to her she felt stupid. He wasn't sleeping, he was…they
were… She shook her head to clear the images crowding
in and pressed a hand to her stomach. Whatever Cesare
and the beautiful Louise were doing could stay behind
closed doors—she didn't want to know.

Taking a deep breath, Anna grabbed her courage
in both hands and knocked. She waited, counting the
seconds, shifting her weight from one bare foot to the
other on the cold stone floor.

Louise had not been serious when she had suggested
tongue in cheek that under the circumstances Cesare
might prefer it if she didn't share his room that night.

'Though, of course, darling, if you're suggesting a
threesome, I'm always up for anything new.'

She had been visibly taken aback, and yes annoyed,
when he had said that actually he did have some work
to do so maybe it might be better if she took a guest
suite for the night. And now, because he'd had a sense

of humour bypass, he was here awake at three a.m. with no prospect of him falling asleep any time soon.

His strong features clenched as he switched off the shower and muttered, 'That damned redhead!'

Having that woman under his roof was taking years off his life and throwing his rigid schedule totally out of kilter.

As he stepped out of the shower Cesare heard the knock. Grabbing a towel from the stack on a hamper, he wound it around his waist as he moved in the direction of the bedroom door. He was not a man who assumed the worst but no one would disturb him at this hour for something that was not an emergency.

Anna's knocks got louder and the gaps between them correspondingly shorter. She was at the point of considering opening the door and yelling when it opened.

She squared her shoulders, mentally prepared. Only it turned out she wasn't!

Who could be, faced with the figure framed in the doorway?

A total sexist pig he might be, but she couldn't imagine anyone, including herself, arguing that Cesare was the sexiest man on the planet. Always effortlessly elegant and immaculate, with water droplets gleaming on his bronzed skin and naked but for a strip of towelling around his narrow hips, Cesare was an image that made her forget why she was here. Hell, at that second she'd have been hard put to remember her name!

He looked down at her with a fierce, almost unfocused expression. His glittering stare had a bone-stripping, soul-baring intensity, but bizarrely it felt as though he wasn't seeing her. He couldn't be; men didn't look at her that way.

'I'm...' She cleared her throat and tried again. 'I'm sorry to disturb you.'

The odd choking sound that emerged from his throat cut her off, then, without a word, he stepped towards her and grabbing her by the waist, he hauled her into him.

Anna was unable to deal with something that couldn't happen again outside her darkest fantasies; something in her brain clicked into off position. She felt an explosion somewhere in her tight chest and stopped breathing. Shock held her immobile. The immobility lasted seconds until her body reacted to the impact of her softness hitting solid bone and muscle—she melted, released a small lost cry into his warm mouth, opening her mouth under the erotic pressure.

Conscious thought vanished, intruding briefly into her world of touch and smell and glorious male hardness. When her shoulder blades ground into the stone wall it hurt but not enough to make her want this to stop. It was enough to enable her to register that she was standing against the wall opposite his open door.

She was sinking and falling into a black hole, into him. Waves of knee-trembling sensation were washing over her, back and forth until they became seamless on a deep, dark maelstrom of wanting.

In a few moments she wouldn't be able to so she had to do it now. From somewhere Anna dredged up enough strength to push him away, hands flat on his chest. She shook her head. How could something so wrong on so many levels feel so damned…so incredibly, gloriously right?

'No.' Once more with feeling, and this time, Anna, say it like you mean it. 'No, I need…' She gasped as his hand slid down her right thigh, then up under the hem of her nightgown.

His glittering eyes swept her face and he smiled. 'I know what you need.'

She shuddered as the words cut like a surgical knife through the layers of pretence. The awful, terrifying part was he did know. He seemed to know exactly what she needed, or at least what she craved. She struggled against his sensual dominance, knowing the moment she accepted it, the moment she gave herself up to the waves of pleasure, it was all over.

Hands flat on his chest, from somewhere she managed to summon up some superhuman strength to push him away one last time.

Cesare's hands went to her elbows as he immediately, casually jerked her back, bringing her body in knee-sagging contact with his lean, hard length. Her vision blurred. His lips were a whisper away from reclaiming hers; she had raised herself up on her toes to meet him halfway. She blurted through lips that didn't feel as if they belonged to her, lips swollen from his kisses, lips that wanted to beg 'don't stop'…

'Jasmine, she's ill…come…you…'

There was a few seconds' delay before he reacted to her inarticulate plea. Cesare blinked and shook his head like someone waking from a dream. His massive chest lifted as he inhaled and he released her.

'Why didn't you say so sooner?' he demanded harshly.

Her jaw dropped at the reprimand.

How was it possible for someone to kiss like that? Touch like that so hotly she could still feel the streaks of fire on her skin, and then sound so terribly cold?

She levered her back from the wall, trying to grab the ties of her robe, but, finding her hands were shaking too much, she settled instead for wrapping her arms around herself. 'You didn't give me much chance.'

The irony seemed wasted on Cesare as he continued to rap out questions. 'Are you sure she was ill? When she's distressed, she has nightmares—'

Arms crossed tightly over her chest, she rubbed her hands vigorously enough over her upper arms to cause a static crackle. She was shaking, her entire body racked by intermittent fine tremors.

Nightmares? Jas wasn't the only one, Anna thought, her voice sharper than normal as she cut across him. 'I'm sure.'

It seemed utterly surreal that they were talking like this. There was absolutely nothing in his behaviour to suggest that moments before he had been about to drag her to his bed. If they'd have got that far. Her heavy-lidded glance slid to her feet, to the floor. She let out a gasp of shame; she would have let him.

Hit by an aftershock tremor stronger than the others, she dug her teeth into her full lower lip and felt a strong surge of self-disgust. Strong, but not strong enough to cancel out the illicit excitement still swirling in her veins like champagne bubbles.

Was that really me?

Cesare dragged a hand through his dark hair and pinned her with an accusing glare. 'Jas is ill and you left her alone?' And appeared at his door at exactly the wrong moment looking like that!

His gaze swept upwards over her bare calves, moving over the kimono-style silky robe that had been belted loosely around her middle and now hung open to reveal an oversized nightshirt that should not have been provocative but was, even if the top button hadn't popped to reveal the promising swell of her satiny smooth, lightly freckled breasts and the shadowy suggestion of cleavage. Even if it had been buttoned up to the neck he would have had no control over the desire that twisted like a molten metal fist in his belly.

Wrong moment!

There was not going to be a right moment for this provocative little witch to appear half dressed at his door. His mistake was attempting to rationalise the attraction that existed. You could not rationalise insanity and that was what this was.

She actually had the nerve to turn those big stricken blue eyes on him like some virginal innocent he'd just defiled. 'Get back to Jas. I'll be there as soon as I get some clothes on.'

And not a moment too soon, Anna thought as he whisked back into the bedroom. Still shaking, she took a deep breath and made some massive allowances for his awfulness. Whatever his faults, he loved his niece. Some people hit out when they were worried. He might be one of them—he might also be a heartless womaniser.

Seconds later he appeared at her side, 'There's no need to panic,' she soothed. 'I don't think it's serious.'

The understanding as much as the suggestion made him see red. 'And what was your medical qualification again?'

She responded through clenched teeth and began to trot to keep up with his long-legged stride. 'By all means blame me if it makes you feel any better, but it is just possible that this is not anyone's fault. Children get tummy aches, they get temperatures, they need a cuddle and six seconds later they get better.'

'Blame you? How could I do that? You're just the innocent victim things happen to. Things like falling into affairs with married men—'

'That's right,' she mumbled. 'Pick out all the high points in my life.' She paused and felt uneasy. If there was such a thing as immersing yourself too deeply in a role, she was guilty of it.

It was legitimate to feel protective of Rosie, but not when she allowed herself to become the victim when she'd only been a helpless observer to what had happened to her cousin.

She was not the one who had lost a baby and very nearly her own life. That was Rosie. That she needed to remind herself of this proved that she had gone way too deep undercover.

'Enough!' Hand on the door leading into Jas's bedroom, Anna stopped and turned around. Pushing her head back against the panelled oak, she tilted it upwards to level her flashing blue eyes on the man whose shoulder she barely reached.

'It's not my fault you've had a row with your girl-friend. Don't take it out on me and don't use me as some sort of substitute. I don't know why and I don't want to,' she declared with a shudder of distaste. 'But I resent being used that way just because I was there.'

'You did not appear to resent it at the time.'

'You didn't give me much chance to do anything, you just...just... I definitely don't want to interview for the job of substitute.' She narrowed her eyes and warned, 'So if you lay a finger on me again I'll...' He'd laid more than a finger and she hadn't wanted him to stop; she'd wanted more. She'd wanted it all. 'Just don't!' she snapped.

Rather to her surprise, after a moment he tilted his head in a jerky motion of assent and retorted, 'Don't turn up at my door half dressed.'

Anna laid her hands on her hot cheeks and schooled her expression into something approaching composure before following him into the room.

Cesare was already at the bedside looking down at his niece. 'So what have you been up to, Angel's little angel?'

'I want Mummy.'

The plaintive note was heartbreaking and Anna could see from Cesare's face that he was not immune. 'I know that, sweetheart. So how are you feeling? Better?'

The little girl thought about it and nodded. 'It was Anna's magic flannel. She wiped my head with it and I felt better. Do you have a magic flannel?'

'All out of magic.'

'A song...the lully song...?' She patted the bed beside her.

The mattress dipped as Cesare arranged his long length on top of the quilt, looking incongruous against the backdrop of pink rabbits.

His expression as their glances connected dared her to comment. 'Pink is your colour.'

Constrained by the presence of his niece, Cesare framed a neutral response. 'If you want anything you know where I am.'

It was a dismissal and one Anna was only too happy to respond to. With a smile for Jasmine and a cold glare for the uncle, she turned to go.

'No, I want you to stay too, Anna.' Jasmine pouted.

Anna turned back with a sigh. 'I don't think there's room. I'll just go and—'

'Here!' Jasmine patted the spot to her right that was not occupied by her uncle. When Anna didn't respond to the imperious direction the childish lips began to quiver. Anna broke at the first tear.

'All right, until you fall asleep I'll just lie here.'

I'm sharing a bed with Cesare Urquart. I bet not many twenty-something virgins can say that! She wondered what he'd say if he knew. Her ex-boyfriend Mark had been astonished and Anna suspected it had been the sheer novelty value of the prospect of having a virgin bride that had made him stop pressuring her for sex.

And she'd been relieved.

When he'd dumped her Mark had made several references to her frigidity in justification and Anna had not thought his comments unfair.

Then Cesare had kissed her.

'No, don't go, don't leave me. Promise?'

Anna, lying rigid, conscious in every cell of her body of the man lying feet away, sighed. 'I promise.'

Jasmine gave a little grunt of satisfaction and looked from her left to her right. 'This is fun.'

Over the child's head the two adults exchanged glances. The gleam of humour she saw in Cesare's drew a reluctant half-smile from Anna before she realised what she was doing and lowered her eyelids and compressed her lips into a straight line. The last thing she wanted to feel for Cesare was a rapport of any sort. It was essential for her to see him, and think of him, as the enemy.

After tonight this was more important than ever. The only way she was going to keep him at a safe distance and avoid any further kissing incidents was by thinking of him as a cold, arrogant automaton.

Didn't do you much good tonight, Anna.

'Sing to me, Uncle Cesare, the song you used to sing to Mummy when she was sad.'

And just when she thought it could not get more surreal Cesare began to sing. He had a good voice, a rich baritone. She didn't understand the Italian words but the tune was soft and soothing.

Anna's eyes drifted closed and when she opened them she was alone in the bed. The clock beside the bed read nine-thirty. She shot from the bed in one horrified leap.

CHAPTER EIGHT

IT WAS NOT his habit to spend the entire night with a woman. He preferred to sleep alone, so watching a woman while she slept was not something Cesare had ever done before.

Last night there had not been a lot else for him to do. He couldn't slip away without the risk of waking Jas, who had crawled into his arms before she fell asleep. He couldn't move, sleep still eluded him, so that left watching the woman sleeping feet away.

It was an alternative to counting sheep.

In repose the lines of wariness disappeared from her face. With her curls of rich auburn she made him think of a sleeping angel. Her face had the look of a carved statue, her skin as fine as alabaster and sprinkled with a dusting of freckles across the bridge of her nose. Her delicate nostrils flared in time with each soft exhalation. Occasionally she would twitch, her blue-veined eyelids fluttering, her breath quickening. What did she dream about when her head thrashed against the pillow?

Was he her nightmare?

Even asleep, her moulded lips were a sensual miracle, a torment, a temptation, an invitation?

It was a long night. By the time Jasmine stirred he could have drawn Anna Henderson's face from memory down to each individual freckle. The idea of sketching her out of his head was appealing but he lacked the talent. His talents lay elsewhere and so did hers. On the brink of reliving that kiss, he pulled back. Some thoughts were not decent with a child in the room. Holding a finger to his lips, he gave Jasmine a conspiratorial wink and nodded towards the sleeping woman.

Jasmine, a bright kid, caught on immediately and entered into the spirit of the game. Totally recovered, she ate an enormous breakfast and then begged to be allowed to go out to the stables to visit the new foal.

He had delivered her to the care of the same groom who had taught him to ride as a child and returned to the house. Entering the hallway, he turned his head in the direction of light footsteps.

'Sorry to disappoint, darling, but it's only me.'

Hard to pretend even to himself that his heart rate hadn't kicked up an expectant beat in the face of Louise's knowing look.

'I was going to ask did you sleep well, but I can see you've had a rough night.'

Cesare, who had no intention of rewarding this fishing expedition, focused on the bags he had not noticed until now stacked by the front door.

'Ah, yes, well, under the circumstances I hope you won't be too heartbroken but I was invited to the party at Crachan. I expect you were too?'

He nodded.

'Well, I knocked them back in favour of your company but given the… Well, I contacted Michael and told him I have an unexpected space in my social diary. You know what they say—one door closes and another opens.' She pressed a kiss to his lips and came up smiling.

Cesare, who appreciated the lack of drama, walked her out to the waiting taxi.

Anna's search had reached the kitchen when her mobile rang. She saw the caller ID and lifted it, heart banging, to her ear.

'Scott?'

'Mother and baby are fine. Annie weighed in at a whopping nine pounds and Rosie sends her love and kisses.'

Anna sighed and gave a happy laugh. 'Oh, that's marvelous. I haven't stopped thinking about you.'

'We can't wait to see you at Christmas. Rosie sends a big kiss.' Scott blew a noisy kiss down the line.

'I can't wait to see you either.' Anna put her mouth to the receiver and blew her own kiss.

Her happy smile lasted until she turned and found herself face to face with a grim-faced Cesare, who was looking very different than he had the previous evening dressed in a stylish designer suit and tie. Not that it was his tailoring that made her stomach contract violently at the unexpected sight of him; it was the aura of masculinity he exuded. It was the primitive instincts that lay just beneath the civilised surface that made her traitorous heart thud harder. It was the memory of that kiss.

She moistened her dry lips and told herself not to look at his mouth.

Naturally she immediately couldn't look any place else. Her memory kicked into panic mode, recalling how it had felt to be on the receiving end of those primitive instincts!

Dear God, what was wrong with her? She'd never had a real conversation with this man. Not one that didn't involve him being nasty and abusive, at any rate, so why did she feel this weird sense of connection?

It was ironic. He'd spent the night in a bed with her and he'd left it feeling more sexually frustrated than he ever had in his entire life. And while he had been lying there suffering, she had presumably been dreaming of this Scott.

For a split second he struggled to control the fresh flare of helpless rage and disgust. The latter was aimed at himself as much as her. He had known what she was so why had the conversation come as such a shocking bolt from the blue? Of course there was a man in the background; the woman hadn't learnt to kiss like that in a convent!

'Good morning.'

His expression didn't change, he simply raised a brow and managed to make her uncomfortably aware of how wrecked she must look with her carelessly scraped-back hair, baggy sweatshirt and joggers.

Presumably it was a version of this look that had people struggling to win his approval. Lucky she wasn't one of them; she didn't need or want his approval. So she'd discovered the previous night that he had a soft spot for his niece? One chink in his armour didn't make him any the less a pain, an arrogant man with an inflated opinion of himself who happened to be able to kiss like… Before she could stop it she was reliving the kiss, remembering how he had tasted.

Her entire body tensed to combat the waves of heat engulfing her. Anna dragged her gaze from his face.

'Sorry.' She bit her lip, irritated by her urge to apologise. What would she be apologising for? Just because he was looking at her as though he thought she had the family silver in her pockets it didn't make her a criminal.

'I was just coming to look for Jas. How is she this morning? You should have woken me.'

'Jas is in the stables feeding the foal. She seems fine. Next time, Miss Henderson, don't wait—inform me the moment she becomes ill.'

His tone made it clear she was not talking to the man who sang the lullaby. She straightened her slender shoulders and lifted her chin, told herself it was totally irrational to let the coldness in his voice hurt.

But it did.

The initial knot of hurt in her chest was giving way to anger as he continued to study her as though she were a bug under a microscope.

She lifted a hand to her hair, knowing she looked as crumpled and dishevelled as he looked sleek and elegant.

'I did come straight away,' she protested. As he was obviously in a vile mood she didn't expect a thank you, but neither did she expect the icy rebuke that came her way. 'She was fine when I put her to bed.'

'It was not your place to say it was fine. It is not fine.'

'I'm s-sorry...'

Was that damned stammer meant to make him feel like some sort of ogre? Was it even real?

'In future run all things to do with Jas's medical treatment past me. Is that clear, Miss Henderson?'

Her chin went up. 'As crystal, Mr Urquart,' she returned, her voice as crisp as the Highland morning and her eyes as sparkling cold as the sea. 'And don't worry, next time I feel the urge to make a decision I will repress it if you will repress the urge to manhandle me.'

On anyone else she might have suspected the lines of colour along his cheekbones signified embarrassment. His magnificent shrug and expression of amused disdain made it clear she'd made the right call.

'No problem, so long as you don't come knocking on my door half dressed at three in the morning.'

She narrowed her eyes. 'Believe me, knocking on your door is the last thing I will be doing. I wouldn't want to have to bring a suit of sexual harassment against you the next time. How is your girlfriend this morning?'

'Louise was called away and I am flying to Rome so I will see you when I return. And, Miss Henderson, if you want to play the sexual harassment card it's a good idea not to stick your tongue down a man's throat. You could as easily be accused of sending mixed bloody messages!'

There was no sign of the fog that had grounded his plane and made the journey back on the motorway, not just boring, but long as he drove through the gated entrance to Killaron. But then the micro climate in the area meant they frequently had different weather patterns from places even a few miles away.

That was half a day he would never get back, and nobody had actually expected him to attend the Rome meeting in person. He knew his sudden last-minute change of decision had created some speculation, resulting in the social media sites being rife with stories of the team's number one driver leaving for a rival team.

Cesare recognised the car as he drove through the gates. He swore and pulled up with a swirl of gravel beside it.

Paul was here? Did that mean he knew that Anna was here? Had she contacted him and he…? Perhaps they had always been in regular contact. Did that mean that the affair had never ended? He felt something twist in his guts in reaction to the possibility.

It was equally possible, though not probable, that this was simply a twist of fate. Was Clare with Paul? Had the mistress already bumped into the wife?

Was he too late to avert a crisis? Short of locking Anna in one of the turrets until he got rid of his unwanted guests, how could he?

Why was he making it his business?

Paul was old enough to look after himself and Anna was not even his employee. He was the one who had not wanted her here, the one who had warned she was trouble, and she was. She was also incredibly sexy. Sexy enough to make a man want to… The muscles in his brown throat contracted as he swallowed. Even if the affair was long over, Paul could take one look at Anna and feel his blood heat to boiling point. One look at Anna was enough to make a man forget he was a married man. What man wouldn't?

Did Paul know about this Scott fellow?

He felt rage rip through him. Why did these men allow her to make fools of them?

Anna sat on the tree stump at the edge of the loch and watched Jas play tug of war with the excited puppy whose feet left the ground as he clung on stubbornly to his end of the branch they fought over.

The child's laughter rang out, making Anna smile, but the sadness stayed in her eyes as she turned her face into the wind, tasting the salt on her lips and breathing in the scent of heather from the hills. She was failing to achieve the sense of serenity this magnificent wild scenery normally gave her.

She would have let it happen.

The knowledge filled her with shame. The memory had a more physical effect, playing havoc with her quivering stomach. She had to focus on the positive. Nothing bad had happened—yet.

This was her own fault. She had let down her defences, something, since that awful night when she had discovered what so-called love could do to a person, she had vowed never to allow.

She would never allow anyone to do to her what that man had done to Rosie.

And now she had.

Not love, of course. She had made a mistake but not

that mistake. She wasn't about to confuse lust for love, though she was a bit more understanding of people who did. The fact was, while she couldn't look at him without thinking about that kiss and going weak with longing, she didn't even like Cesare. Her feelings for him were not solid, not real. She could wake up tomorrow, look at him and think, What did I ever see in him?

Beyond a perfect face and an incredible body that could launch a thousand fantasies...

Her lips tightened as she felt the hurt knot in her belly tighten. This morning he'd acted as if it had never happened, then he had all but accused her of asking for it!

Even when Mark had dumped her she hadn't felt vulnerable. Let down certainly, and, yes, slightly foolish—well, it was kind of ironic. She had thought she had her life sorted.

She hadn't been sitting around waiting for some white knight who would turn out to be a total sleaze. She had allowed a computer to find her a man who represented safe solidity, a man who, like her, thought a marriage based on mutual respect and common interest stood more chance of surviving than something based on a transient chemical reaction. And he had dumped her, if not at the altar then embarrassingly close to it, for, of all things, a six-feet-tall lingerie model—a real meeting of minds!

If this was about sex, maybe she ought to get it over with...

She shook her head. Sleep with Cesare? The flaws in that plan hit her immediately, the main being that he wouldn't be interested unless he'd just had a row with his girlfriend. She was under no illusions that a man like Cesare, with his well-known penchant for leggy blondes, would, under normal circumstances, give her a second glance. A lovers' tiff was the only thing that explained the woman's absence from his room.

Cesare was still swearing in two languages when the door opened before he reached it.

He clamped his lips closed. During his short but meteoric driving career he had been renowned for his ability to maintain his cool under any and all circumstances. Labelled enigmatic by the press and a machine by his envious rivals, at that moment he found himself struggling to contain his feelings, and if his housekeeper's expression was any indication he was not doing a very good job.

He tilted his head in stiff acknowledgement of Mrs Mack, and, not trusting himself to speak without yelling, raised a sable eyebrow in enquiry.

'Mr Dane is in the library.'

Cesare struggled not to read too much into her air of tight-lipped disapproval. His housekeeper disapproved of many things, not just discovering a married guest in a passionate clinch with an employee. Even so the image that tortured him remained in his head, making him break into a jog before he reached the library door, where he stopped and took a deep breath.

Paul turned out to be alone. The only thing he had been getting close and friendly with, if the levels in the bottle were any indication, was his whisky. Cesare had no problem sharing booze, but when it came to his...

A frown tugged his brow into furrows. What was she other than not his?

Not his, but a total nightmare and she was not getting paid to sleep with his married friend, so his attitude was totally justified.

'This is a surprise, Paul.' Despite an effort to inject some warmth Cesare didn't even manage tepid.

The other man didn't appear to notice the lack of tepid.

Cesare took a deep breath and decided against small talk. Better to know straight off how bad this could get.

On the plus side, if there was a plus side, the sight of the family unit in the flesh might bring home to Anna that her actions had an impact on others.

Or it might drive her back into her married lover's arms.

'Is Clare with you? The children?' If so he would have to be especially nice to Mrs Mack, who had threatened—not seriously—early retirement after the twin boys' last stay.

Paul, in the act of topping his glass, raised it to Cesare and shook his head. 'Clare has left me… Acshully,' he slurred, 'she has thrown me out.'

Cesare froze as the alarm bells in his head became deafening.

'She found out about Rosanna?'

Had Paul confessed?

Cesare discarded this possibility. Paul was not the confessing kind. He was the kind to dump his problem on his friends and expect them to sort them for him. How many times over the past five years had they played this scene? Cesare experienced a flash of guilt at the thought and his irritation. He owed Paul.

And Paul knew it.

His friend was going to carry on dumping his problems. What did the psychologists call it—learnt behaviour?

Paul gave a hazy frown and blinked. 'Are you all right ? You look…' He gave a sudden light-bulb grin. 'Rosanna. You mean Rosie, the delicious Rosie. So, so sweet…so…so hot. Just the best.'

Cesare's lips thinned into a grimace of distaste. At his sides his hands clenched into fists as he ground his teeth audibly and fought his way through a red-mist moment.

'No, she never found out about Rosie, but Rosie, she was different, the real thing. I wish…' He gave an emotional sigh. 'No, this was nothing. A one-night stand, that's all.' He dismissed it with a snap of his fingers before he took another gulp of thirty-year-old malt. 'But Clare won't see that. She won't listen to reason at all,' he whined.

He paused as if expecting a sympathetic murmur in response to the petulant complaint, but when it didn't come he took another gulp of whisky.

'I hoped you might make her see reason, Cesare. She likes you. You've got a way with women.'

'That's not "a way", it's called not cheating.'

Before Paul could respond the door opened, letting in the distant sounds of Jas's laugher, dogs' excited barking and Anna, who walked into the room in a mood for a fight. It didn't take any intuitive skills to know this; every delicious inch of her screamed it.

Cesare, following instinct rather than logic, moved to block her from Paul's view.

A view that, mad or not, was well worth looking at— and Cesare did! The tight jeans emphasised the tight curves of her delicious bottom and the fluffy sweater, a shade slightly lighter than her eyes, bore a slogan across the chest that invited the observer to save the forest for the future. Cesare considered the chances of any man reading that instruction and thinking about trees fairly negligible.

'Can this wait?' Her face was bare of all but the lightest dusting of make-up, but it was tinged pink and glowing from the fresh air. She looked sexily wholesome.

Anna's delicate jaw tightened. 'I'm so sorry to disturb you but I saw your car and realised you were back,' she remarked in a voice that dripped insincerity like honey. 'But as you want all major decisions run by you I thought I'd better consult you. We bumped into Samantha and her mum while we were walking the dogs and they invited Jas to a sleepover. I explained I'd have to check with you as I'm only the babysitter and I wouldn't want to exceed my authority.'

'Yes, fine.'

Anna's jaw dropped; the anticlimax was intense. She felt like someone all dressed up with nowhere to go. 'Fine?'

'Yes, fine.'

'But—' She stopped. What did she want from him? Rudeness, anger? Bottom line she realised that what she was asking for was to be noticed by Cesare. Being ignored hurt a lot more than cross words or insults.

When did she get this pathetic and needy? she asked herself in disgust.

'Is that all?' he rasped impatiently.

She took a deep breath and huffed it out slowly, then, with a shrug she hoped matched his indifference, tipped her head. It was crazy to be hurt because he had better things to do than argue the toss with her.

'Yes, fine, I'll let them know.' Focusing on a point beyond his shoulder now, she caught a movement.

Cesare, arms folded across his chest, took a step towards her. 'That will be all, Miss Henderson.'

The peculiar intensity of his harsh tone brought her attention back to his face. As she noticed for the first time the lines of tension that bracketed his mouth her brow furrowed. Were this and the accompanying general taut quality of his tense body language connected with Louise? Had the row she had taunted him with been serious? Were his intentions towards the blonde serious?

Neither possibility gave her much pleasure, just a horrible sick feeling low in her belly. Before she could analyse it a figure rose to his feet from the sofa and moved with the over-cautious gait of someone not quite sober towards the open bottle on the bureau, glass in hand.

Slightly to her right, she didn't need to see Cesare just outside the periphery of her vision to feel the tension flowing off him in waves.

'Oh, sorry.' Feeling awkward, she flashed a look towards Cesare that just stopped short of being an apology. 'I didn't know you had company.'

Cesare took a step towards her, the expression on his face as he moved from her to his mystery guest odd. She couldn't put a name to it. Had she just interrupted a crucial moment in a business deal? Not likely, considering the measure of whisky the stranger was pouring into his glass, but it was clear from the atmosphere that she was intruding.

'I'll go and help Jas pack her bag.'

'You do that.'

Cesare waited until the door closed.

'What the hell was that about?'

'What about?'

'Anna.'

'Rose—I think she was the love of my life. If Clare hadn't been pregnant... I told Rose if she wanted to keep the baby I'd help, though maybe it was for the best that she lost it.'

'She was pregnant?'

'Probably a false alarm.'

'You didn't go to the trouble of finding out?'

'Clean break, you said. The girl...red hair...I suppose she does look like Rose,' he conceded. 'I admit for a split second there I thought that girl was Rosie.'

Cesare gritted his teeth, frustrated by this display of ignorance on both their parts. 'That girl is Rosanna Henderson.'

Paul focused his bleary glance, tilting his head to look up at his taller friend before he slopped down on the leather sofa. 'Quite a coincidence, but she's not my Rose. My Rosie was taller, slimmer, figure like a wand,' he recalled. 'And no freckles, skin like a pearl.'

Finding himself on the point of defending, even waxing lyrical on, the subject of Anna's skin, which was to his mind several shades above perfect, Cesare stopped. What was he saying? Paul was drunk but not that drunk. For the first time he began to consider the crazy possibility that the ignorance on both their parts wasn't faked.

'You are saying that you did not have an affair with the woman who just came in here?' He mentally tried out explanations. Even his razor-sharp instincts could not begin to unpick this maze.

Paul shook his head, then grinned. 'But given the chance—'

He never reached the end of the sentence; instead he found himself standing up against a wall. His friend, not looking very friendly at all, still holding his collar in both fists.

He held up both hands, slopping the drink he still held. 'S-sorry, didn't mean to tread on your toes. I should have remembered you always did have a thing about redheads,' he mused, giving a shaky laugh. 'The headmaster's daughter? If I hadn't covered for you that night when we were in…the sixth form or fifth…? If you'd have been caught—'

Cesare looked at his friend and shook his head. How long had he been making excuses for the other man? How long had he been tolerating behaviour that he would have been the first to condemn in someone else? With a snort of disgust he released Paul, who staggered backwards.

'Hell, man, what's got into you?'

'I grew up. I suggest you do the same.'

The coldness in Cesare's voice made the other man blink, but he nodded amenably. 'Of course, of course, you're right. Tell me what to do. I need Clare and the kids…'

Cesare shook his head and asked himself how many times he had responded to that request. What had Angel called it? Enabling? How come his little sister had seen what he hadn't? 'How old was this Rosie when you had an affair, Paul?'

The other man responded to the question with a petulant half-resentful shrug. 'I don't know.'

'I think you do.'

'Around twenty, I think.'

'Around twenty as in nineteen?'

'She was very mature.'

Cesare had an overwhelming urge to shake his friend until his teeth rattled. Instead he dug his hands into his pockets as he strode across the room to the old-fashioned bell pull, which he yanked hard.

'Mrs Mack will get you a taxi.'

A look of utter astonishment crossed the other man's face. 'You're sending me away? Not going to help me? But what will I do?'

'Your mess, Paul, you figure it out.' He delivered the long-overdue tough love and found it a lot easier than he had anticipated. On cue, the housekeeper bustled into the room. 'Mrs Mack, Mr Dane will be needing a taxi to the village.'

Paul reached out his hand, touching the taller man's arm. 'But, Cesare—' A glance from Cesare's hooded eyes made his hand fall from his sleeve.

'One suggestion, Paul—stop thinking of yourself as the victim here. You're not—Clare and the kids are. The girl you charmed is. So show a little of the guts you showed when you risked your life diving into that swollen river to pull me out of the car.' At the door he turned back. 'You have what many men would give a lot to have.' He might not be one of them, but Cesare knew many who would have swapped places with Paul in a heartbeat. 'Good luck, Paul,' he added, meaning it. 'You're a lucky man. I hope you wake up and realise how lucky before it's too late.'

'What if it already is?' For the first time there was genuine fear in the other man's voice.

CHAPTER NINE

JASMINE HAD RANSACKED several drawers in her bedroom in her search for the pair of pyjamas she wanted to take with her for the sleepover. The contents now lay in a brightly coloured jumble on the bedroom floor.

Having waved goodbye to the excited little girl, Anna set about picking up the crumpled items of clothing. Then, after smoothing the pretty quilt and plumping up the pile of cushions, she closed the door behind her and with a sigh leaned against it.

Rather than welcoming the relaxing evening that lay ahead, Anna found herself dreading it. Time to think with no distractions was something she definitely didn't want.

She had told herself that she wouldn't think about Cesare's weird behaviour, but how could she not? With the rest of the evening to herself, what else did she have to do?

She walked around the room twitching a tartan throw that didn't need twitching, punching a cushion, then, instead of putting it back on the sofa, walking over to the deep mullioned window with it clutched to her chest. Her expression abstracted, she stared down at the manicured lawn below, allowing her gaze to move beyond the grounds to the monumental craggy mountains that stood out against a rare blue sky.

First his easy capitulation, then the thing with the guest—she hadn't really registered the man's face, just Cesare's obvious reluctance to introduce them. Now that she thought about it he had virtually thrown her out of the room. What did he think she was going to do?

She had nothing but the wall to vent her anger on and the twelve inches of solid stone absorbed her angry glare much the way her intended target would have. The man had the thickest skin... Skin... She shook her head to clear the tactile sensations that made her fingers curl as she thought of Cesare's satiny dark gold-toned skin.

Was he even now recounting details of her imagined sleazy past to his friend? Hating the fact that the possibility had the power to hurt her, she walked across to the table and picked up a book she had started reading earlier that week. She had flopped down into a high-backed easy chair when without warning the door opened.

She had stopped pretending even to herself that the sight of him didn't turn her into a drooling idiot. In her defence there was good reason: Cesare was a beautiful sexy predator, the sort that didn't have to lift a finger to capture his victims—they were lining up to be eaten.

And to her intense shame, she was no different.

She laid her book down and sat forward, her spine straight as she levelled a condemnatory glare up at his face. 'I thought this was meant to be a private wing?'

He was still wearing what she privately called his professional uniform, one of the slickly tailored designer suits that he must have dozens of, minus the usual silk tie and plus a heavy shadow of stubble on his angular jaw.

'You expect me to knock in my own house?'

Her husky little laugh sent a flash of heat down his body.

'I expect you to do exactly what you want,' she admitted bitterly.

'If that were true you'd be naked and under me.'

The glitter in his deep-set hooded eyes as much as the raw pronouncement drew a gasp from Anna, who, despite the heart-racing excitement swirling like champagne bubbles through her veins, adopted a stiff expression and demanded, 'Am I meant to find that statement a turn-on?' Because if so it worked, oh, big time it worked!

'Not my intention, just a fringe benefit, but leaving that to one side—'

He made it sound the easiest thing in the world, which for him it probably was, while his comment had left her shaking with lust. Her nervous system was in meltdown but Anna, by some superhuman effort, managed to hide it behind a rigid mask of composure as she focused her eyes on a point over his left shoulder.

'I'm puzzled.'

Anna's gaze swung back to his face as she widened her eyes in an attitude of mock wonder. 'I'm amazed. I thought you knew everything.'

He responded to the bitter jibe with a tight smile. 'If you had an affair with Paul Dane why didn't you recognise him when you walked into the library and saw him sitting there?'

He watched as a look of blank astonishment washed over Anna's face. In a matter of seconds the colour leeched from her face and then rushed back, staining her skin pink.

'That man was Paul Dane?'

She had smiled at him.

Her hands balled into fists. Smiled! She should have punched his lights out. Her blue-eyed fury switched to the person delivering the information.

'You invited him here?' she choked. 'You thought that was funny?' Rising from the sofa, she was forced back down by the large hands on her shoulders.

Cesare sank down with her. Lifting his hands from her shoulders, he took her hands in his, drawing them onto the hard contours of his muscular thighs.

'Let me go.' She had the opportunity to tell that slimy rat exactly what she thought of him and nothing and nobody was going to stop her.

'Certainly, when you have told me what the hell this is about,' he retorted calmly.

'I'm not staying a night, not a second, under the same roof as that man,' she declared in a shaking voice.

Cesare had been trying to break through her defensive rigidity, but success was not sweet. The pain shimmering in her beautiful eyes was painful to witness. 'He isn't.'

She lifted eyes that glowed with angry contempt to his face. 'Isn't what, a total scumbag?' She loosed a wild laugh tinged with bitterness. 'Well, your definition is clearly different from mine.'

'Under this roof.'

It took a few seconds before her brow puckered and she responded with a subdued, 'Oh.' Before adding, 'But the principle is the same.'

His platinum gaze scanned her face. 'You're not leaving.'

Unable not to challenge the confidence in this statement, she lifted her chin. 'Oh, and why is that?'

Talk about an own goal. She lowered her lashes and thought, Never ask a question when you don't want to hear the true answer. He had to know that she spent each moment of each day anticipating a glimpse of him with as much dread as longing; the only thing she hated more than seeing him was not seeing him.

Fully expecting to hear him expose her weakness, because he had to know, she was shocked to hear him say something quite different.

'You wouldn't leave Angel in the lurch. You have too many principles.' His wolfish grin flashed, humour warming the metallic hardness of his eyes. 'And anyway you're way too stubborn.'

Cesare found her ability to bring a fight-to-the-death mentality to even the most innocuous discussion one of the most irritating and exhausting things about her, but then Anna, if that was her name, did manage to press all his buttons, frequently at the same time.

Given her irritant status a sensible man would have responded to her threat to leave with a sigh of relief, but then a sensible man, Cesare conceded, would not have allowed her to become an obsession. The word was not, he realised, an exaggeration. *Dio,* the sooner he took this woman to bed, the sooner he might get, not just his life, but his mind back! He had no idea yet where she fitted into this story but the important thing was she had not been Paul's mistress. So he knew who she wasn't, but not who she was.

'Don't be so sure,' she muttered, trying not to be ridiculously pleased by the back-handed compliment and trying not to inhale too obviously his warm, male, musky fragrance, but he smelt so good!

'Right now explanation.'

The clipped instruction made her blink. 'What?' Anna asked, struggling to focus thanks to the brown thumb now stroking the sensitive inside of her wrist. Ironically he didn't even seem to be aware he was doing it, while the contact was sending sharp breath-stealing electric thrills through her entire body.

'Explain to me why you pretended to be someone you are not.'

She got the strength from somewhere to tug her hands free. Experiencing a stab of disappointment when he didn't attempt to retrieve them, she folded them in her lap and shuffled her bottom to the far end of the sofa.

The gesture drew a brief wry smile from Cesare, but his eyes remained intent and unsmiling on her. Face turned to him in half profile, exposing the smooth curve of her cheek and the elegant line of her long neck, at times like this she frequently brought to mind one of those Degas dancing figures, combining sinuous, sensuous promise with an almost ethereal quality, but she was warm to touch with an earthy sensuality that no painting could reproduce.

'I'm exactly who I said I was—Anna Henderson.' Her eyes flickered to him and then she felt her anger slip quickly away again. There had been occasions recently when she had lost sight of that fact, times when she had caught herself asking, Is this me?

There were moments when the woman who had caught the sleeper from London just a short time ago seemed like a stranger, one who had felt a lot more sure of things than she was.

'You have never had an affair with Paul.'

The accusation in his voice made her turn her head sharply, causing her hair to whip across her face. Blowing the gleaming strands from her cheek, she tucked them impatiently behind her ears.

'So this is the mind they liken to a steel trap in action? Wow, I'm overcome with admiration.'

He arched a sardonic brow and drawled, 'Sometimes, Anna, your efforts to derail a discussion are pretty pathetic.'

The boredom in his voice brought a flush to her cheeks. 'Not unlike your selective amnesia. I never said I'd had an affair with him,' she reminded him bitterly. 'That was all your idea.'

'An idea you did nothing to dispel.' The furrow in his brow deepened as he recalled the level of genuine animosity in her voice when he had mentioned Paul's name, yet it was now clear they were strangers.

'You've obviously never met Paul, so how come you had such a strong reaction when I mentioned his name?'

'You mean like you do, I jump to conclusions?' She shook her head, sidetracked from the question by her feelings of angry resentment. 'You know, I really do believe that you take some sort of twisted pleasure in thinking the worst of me,' she accused, remembering all those occasions when his eyes had held contempt when he had looked at her. Though his contempt was easier to cope with than the... She lowered her eyes, swallowing hard. Even the memory of his burning stare could make her insides shudder.

Naked and under me.

He really had said it. And the words had carried all the hallmark of compulsion.

Anna knew all about compulsion. Bringing her eyelashes down in a concealing sweep, she wrapped her arms around herself, but the instinctive protective action did not protect her from anything. She felt wide open and exposed, her feelings so close to the surface that she shook with the effort of maintaining a façade of control.

Having now experienced forbidden lust, she felt guilty, because although she had always said the right supportive things to Rosie, no matter how hard she had tried not to judge, secretly she had wondered how her cousin could allow herself to fall for the man who had wrecked her life. Rosie wasn't stupid; she was smart and beautiful. She could have any man so why choose one who belonged to someone else and believe every lie he told?

It had seemed utterly incomprehensible to Anna, who knew that she would never allow herself to want someone unsuitable. Yet here she was, looking at the embodiment of unsuitable and wanting…wanting so badly that she ached with it. She dreamed that want, she breathed it and she was utterly exhausted trying to pretend it wasn't there!

Giving her head a dazed shake, she unwound the fingers that had somehow got tangled with his and snatched them away, laying her hands primly in her lap. Unlike Rosie she wasn't being lied to and unlike Rosie she was going to protect herself.

'What else was I meant to think? Your name…' His voice thickened as his eyes lifted to her burnished head. 'I saw you, your hair—' he shook his head and dragged a hand through his own dark hair. 'It was obviously not you, but you looked so alike. You looked like the girl I saw with Paul in the restaurant and you didn't deny it!'

Anna's slender shoulders hunched as her attitude of defiance fell away. Enough was enough—he'd find out the truth with or without her help. 'It wasn't my story to tell. Rosie swore me to secrecy. No one else knows about any of it.'

The tension in his shoulders relaxed slightly. At last they were getting somewhere. 'Is Rosie your sister?' That would explain the likeness, the similarity in colouring.

'As good as—she's my cousin but we were brought up together. Aunt Jane and Uncle George became my guardians after my parents…the accident, but we couldn't be closer if we had been sisters.'

'I did not know you were an orphan.'

'Why would you?'

'And the name?'

'I'm Rosanna and she's Rosemary. I get called Anna and she gets Rosie. She's the last person in the world you would imagine having an affair with a married man,' she told him fiercely.

'And where do you come into this? I'm not judging your cousin. I just want the facts.'

But Cesare was judging her. Anna had tricked him. Had she been laughing while he…? He clenched his teeth. He needed to stop blaming her for what was his massive error of judgment.

Again she displayed her startling ability to tune into his thoughts. 'You judged me;' she hit back bitterly before lowering her gaze to hide the sudden rush of tears that she blinked rapidly to disperse.

The glistening point of moisture sliding down her cheek made his chest tighten. He lowered the hand he had reached out to blot it and said roughly, 'I thought you didn't give a damn what I think of you.' No one in a long time had challenged him the way this tiny little redhead had.

Her head came up at the charge. 'I don't.' She bit her quivering lip and sniffed angrily. 'But I won't have you sneering at Rosie,' she told him fiercely.

'I'm not looking for a target. I'm looking for explanations.' He clenched his jaw and struggled to control his impatience. 'My best friend just came to ask me for help and I showed him the door. I think that entitles me to a little information.'

Anna's eyes widened, some of her anger falling away as her blue gaze lifted in startled enquiry to his face. 'You sent him away?' she probed. She couldn't imagine what had happened to make Cesare act this way to the man whose cause he had championed so robustly. A man he had been determined to think the innocent victim.

'Because it's time to break the cycle, because I'm his friend and I owe him a debt, one I can never repay.' It was the right call but it wasn't easy.

Anna struggled to make sense of his comment. 'He lent you money?' While she had had the impression from Rosie that her ex lover was not a poor man, she had not got the idea that he was in the same league as Cesare, but then who was?

'There was a period in my life after I learnt I would never drive again professionally that I...' His sooty lashes swept downwards, concealing his eyes from her as he delivered a dry smile. 'Let's just say that adrenaline is addictive and I took some risks.'

Anna, recognising an understatement when she heard it, went icy cold. The images the comment evoked made the hairs on her nape stand on end.

'I had taken delivery of a new car that day and... Was I trying to prove something?'

It seemed to Anna, who watched as he shrugged, his lips curving into a self-contemptuous smile as he considered the motivation of his younger self, that he was almost talking to himself, asking himself the questions, not her.

'Well, either way, I took a tight bend too fast—something an amateur or a boy racer would do—and ended in a river. I took a blow to the head and lost consciousness.'

The blow to the head had resulted in the bleed on the brain that had necessitated the doctors operating to relieve the pressure. The full, utter selfishness of his action had been brought home to him when Angel told him later that the doctors had been unable to confirm until he had woken up with the mother of all headaches that there would be no permanent brain damage.

Anna pressed a hand to her stomach and swallowed. Her reaction to this story was physical.

'But you did get out.' Stupid question, Anna. He was sitting here looking very much alive. In fact the most alive person she had ever met; his vitality had a combustible quality.

For once he let her stupidity pass without comment. 'Paul happened to be following behind. We'd been friends at school but lost touch and gone in different directions. If we hadn't then bumped into each other in the casino the previous evening, who knows? He saw it all and didn't hesitate. He dived in and fished me out.'

Anna released a shuddering breath and abandoned her hunched defensive position. It was hardly surprising, given the story, that he had been so stubborn in championing his friend.

'That was brave of him.'

The dark brooding expression in his silvered eyes became gently mocking as they swept her face. 'I thought he was a monster?'

'Not a monster, just selfish and cruel, but even monsters are capable of bravery on occasion, I admit that.

Your friend saved your life.' And had been milking it ever since, she speculated, finding charity hard to come by when it came to this man. 'But he almost took Rosie's.'

Cesare arched a brow, his stormy grey eyes narrowing to slits. 'Isn't that a little dramatic? Broken hearts are rarely fatal.'

His mockery hit her on the raw and the bitter words were out before she could check them. 'When a bottle of painkillers and half a bottle of vodka are involved they can be.'

An awful realisation hit Cesare. 'Your cousin attempted to take her life?'

Regretting her words, Anna leaned towards him, reaching out in a gesture of unconscious fluttering appeal. 'I shouldn't have said anything. Nobody knows. Not her parents, not anyone,' she told him urgently.

She appeared to think it likely that he was about to expose her cousin's secret. Cesare swallowed the insult and tore his eyes off the fluttering hand that had somehow got itself sandwiched between his two.

How did that happen?

As the small hand curled tight within his, Cesare was conscious of an emotional response shaking loose in his belly. It was anger, he decided, anger that the older cousin had selfishly placed this burden of secrecy on Anna's shoulders. Admittedly Rosie had been young at the time but that meant that Anna had been even younger.

Her eyes remained on his but Cesare had the impression it was not him she was seeing as she began to recite in a strange monotone flatness a story that he assumed she had never told anyone.

'I was still living at home. Rosie had her first flat. I was really envious,' she recalled with a sad reminiscent smile. 'I'd arranged to go that night to pick up some...' She shook her head and slid a sideways glance at Cesare; his expression told her nothing. 'That doesn't matter, but she'd forgotten I was coming and...' Her voice faded as she saw the scene again, the pills scattered over the table, the vodka spilled. The air had been thick with a sour smell—Rosie had been violently sick at one point, a circumstance which, according to the staff in the casualty department, had saved her from any long-term damage.

It was while she had sat with Rosie in the hospital cubicle, a thin curtain separating them from the chaos of a busy Saturday night of an inner-city casualty unit, waiting for the psychiatric consult the hospital insisted on before they would discharge her, that she heard the full story. Rosie had known it was wrong because he was married but she loved him and he loved her. He had told her so often and he was so wonderful.

It turned out the wonderful man discovered he couldn't leave his wife, who was expecting their first child. A week later Rosie had discovered that she was too.

'When she lost the baby—'

His sharp intake of breath made her turn her head. 'Your cousin really was carrying Paul's child? He said...'

Anna tipped her head, her smooth brow pleating into

a sad, contemplative frown. 'She found out just after he left her. She didn't think he believed her. Afterwards she just told him she lost it, no details, it was just a text.'

Cesare bit back the exclamation on his tongue, not wanting to interrupt her halting narrative. Any lingering guilt that he had sent his friend away vanished.

'I think Rosie thought the miscarriage was her punishment for briefly considering a termination.' She scanned his face and, seeing no evidence of the rush to judgment she had anticipated, lowered her defences a little. 'If only she'd spoken to someone, but she didn't. She was too ashamed to tell her parents. She felt it was all her fault. She still loved him.'

Cesare listened to the level of pain and the depth of emotion in her voice, and wondered how he could ever have thought her capable of the actions he had accused her of.

'She lost the baby. She was all alone and then she came back home to the flat.'

'It was at this time she attempted to take her own life?' And he had considered Paul the victim.

Anna nodded, unable to look at him as she struggled to govern her emotions. She heard him swear. 'I had a key. I let myself in. There were pills on the table and drink. Luckily she'd been sick. The hospital said if I'd been a little bit later...' She closed her eyes, aware as she sat there with her head in her hands of his footsteps on the wooden floor.

'Drink this.'

She opened her eyes and shook her head, her nose

wrinkling in response to the smell of the contents of the glass he held out to her.

'I don't like spirits,' she said through chattering teeth.

'You will feel better.'

'You're a bully,' she accused, curling her fingers around the glass. Her eyes met his over the rim as he watched her take a sip then shudder. 'It's horrible,' she complained without heat. The glow was making its way down her throat and pooling in her belly. She had stopped shaking. 'It was all a long time ago.'

The indent between his dark brows deepened as he studied her face.

'Good girl,' he commended as he retook his seat. It was obvious the memory of discovering her cousin had left its mark on Anna.

Anna choked a little. 'That's the nicest thing you've ever said to me.' She felt her eyes fill with emotional tears and blinked madly. She didn't want him to run away with the crazy idea she'd been waiting for a word of praise from him.

'Slowly,' Cesare advised, touching the glass that was pressed to her lips.

She nodded and even managed a realistic little cough to reinforce the idea raw alcohol was responsible for her tears, not raw emotion.

'So how did your cousin's parents take it when they found out?' His eyes narrowed as he contemplated his own response. In that father's place he would have hunted down the man responsible. Of course if the girl had been as stubbornly mute as Angel had been that was not easy—at least Angel had come to him. For that he would remain eternally grateful.

'They never did—she didn't tell them and she swore me to secrecy. I suppose other than Scott I'm the only person who knows.'

He stiffened at the name. 'Scott?' A man she felt close enough to share her cousin's secrets with.

Anna smiled and sniffed as she fumbled for a tissue and found none up the sleeve of her top. 'Her husband.'

The relief he felt was so intense that his entire body slumped.

'Rosie got married last year. Scott is Canadian—they moved to Toronto. Aunt Jane and Uncle George have gone over to be there with her for the birth of her and Scott's baby, who was born yesterday…a little girl called Annie.'

Cesare swallowed, struggling to acknowledge the jealousy that had caused him to rush to judgment as he handed her a tissue and watched as she blew her small nose. It had never occurred to him that it was possible for such a prosaic action to trigger a rush of gut emotion. While recognising it he stopped short of identifying that visceral tightening as tenderness.

He ground his teeth as he asked himself why. Why would he be surprised? From the outset his reaction to her had been unlike that to any other woman, totally disproportionate even if she had been the woman he had wanted to believe her to be.

And yes, he acknowledged he had wanted to, but why? It was hard to discount the possibility that there had been an element of self-protection—some might call it cowardice and they'd be right—in his eagerness to believe she lacked any morals. He had needed her to be the sort of woman any sensible man would avoid involvement with.

That much, at least, had not changed. Cesare needed to control his feelings with women, needed to keep his emotions separate from sex. The ability to walk away without regret was important to him. That was why he only allowed himself to be involved with women he could not hurt, women who knew the score, women who could not hurt him. *Dio*, I'm the king of shallow, he thought with a grunt of self-disgust.

But it was who he was.

Even after these revelations essentially nothing had changed. Anna Henderson had stepped out of the box he had put her in but she still remained off limits. Possibly more so than previously. She was everything he avoided in a woman; she was not the sort of lover for whom a diamond bracelet would ease the pain of separation. Anna Henderson had been acting the part of a woman who invested emotionally in a sexual relationship because she hadn't been acting; she was the sort of woman he didn't go within a mile of.

One barrier lowered and another lifted. A man just had to go with the flow. It might be easier if he could stop thinking of her underneath him, her lovely legs wrapped around him. He cleared his throat.

'So the story has had a happy ending.' At least for the victim that he had been so eager to condemn. He suspected that the trauma of watching her cousin driven to the brink of utter despair by a man had left a few scars for her impressionable young cousin.

Some man would need to work hard to earn her trust—some man, but not him.

Then it hit him like the proverbial bolt from the blue: the 'scared virgin afraid of her own sexual impulses' act was not an act either—it was what she was!

The truth had been staring him in the face. There had been dozens of clues. How had he managed not to see it until now?

Opening his clenched fists, he took her chin between his long fingers and brought her face up to him. 'You have never had a lover.' Despite his efforts he could not keep the accusation from his voice.

Did she have it tattooed across her forehead or something? With an angry, embarrassed growl she snatched her chin from his fingers. He was looking at her as though she had two heads.

Anna cleared her throat and observed bitterly, 'Don't worry, it's not contagious.' Was she meant to apologise or something?

His jaw clenched. 'Why the hell didn't you say something?'

'I really don't see how my frigidity affects my ability to do my job!'

'I'm not your employer, as you never cease to remind me, and...' He took a deep breath, his eyes darkening as they fastened on her face. 'And you are nothing that even faintly resembles frigid!' he blasted.

The raw comment caused everything inside Anna to dissolve, the denial of her feelings washed away along with the rush of jumbled emotions. The deluge drew a fractured sigh from her parted lips.

Her lashes lying in a dark protective filigree against the flush of her smooth cheeks, she listened to the series of colourful bilingual curses.

Then silence.

CHAPTER TEN

TOSSING AND TURNING, replaying the conversation in her head, Anna lasted until one a.m., at which point she switched on the bedside lamp and, pushing her feet into a pair of slippers, padded through to Angel's sitting room.

Switching on the television for background noise, she went into the adjoining kitchen to warm some milk. Catching her reflection in the mirrored surface of a cabinet, she winced. Several disturbed nights had left their mark. The circles under her eyes were dark purple.

Carrying her drink back, she curled up on the sofa. She was halfway through the mug of cocoa before she tuned into the programme that was playing in time to see terror on the faces of people on the ground as they watched a person strapped to a parachute hurtle towards the ground. Their cheer when it inflated at the very last minute was echoed by the trio of presenters sitting in the studio.

'A worthy number four, I'm sure you'll agree. And now the crash survivor voted number three by the viewers was—'

Anna didn't want to know. With a sound of disgust

she picked up the remote, grimacing at the exploitative nature of the programme. How long before they were compiling lists about fatal crashes?

In her eagerness to change the channel she hit the wrong button and instead of switching channels the volume went up to a deafening level in time for her to hear the presenter's reveal, 'Cesare Urquart. Who among us can forget the famous crash that ended his driving career?'

Hand extended towards the television, Anna froze as the sound of cars screeching around the track through driving rain filled the screen. A second later the scene was transformed into a wet version of hell as the car being lapped swerved, causing the one behind to hit it. The second car sailed into the air before landing yards away upside down...then just as Anna was about to breathe again more cars ploughed into the second car, one after the other until nothing was left but a twisted mass of metal. Then unbelievably from the twisted mass a figure appeared. He climbed out of the wreckage, took several steps before pulling off his helmet and crumpling to the ground, just as the wreckage exploded sending a fireball into the air. It was at that point that the emergency vehicles that had arrived en masse then cut the solitary figure off from the camera's lens until he reappeared on a stretcher. Anna couldn't take her eyes off the seemingly lifeless hand that skimmed the ground, leaving a trail of blood.

The presenter was speaking again, his magnified voice bouncing off the walls of the room, but Anna didn't hear what he was saying. Her eyes were welded to the screen. She couldn't even blink as they replayed the crash, this time in slow, sickening motion that magnified each horrific blood-chilling moment.

It was the loud imperative banging on the door that enabled her to break the connection with the screen. She was shaking her head just as Cesare walked into the room, still dressed in the same clothes he had been wearing earlier. He was looking a lot less pristine, though, even with his jaw dusted with a thick layer of stubble, his cropped dark hair standing up in spiky tufts and his eyes slightly bloodshot, he managed to put the sexy into haggard.

'What the hell is going on? You've woken half the building.' A slight exaggeration, actually a massive exaggeration. The thickness of the walls meant that it was unlikely anyone but him had heard the blast of noise emanating from the apartment, unless that person had been sleepwalking along the corridor just below.

After the silence of the previous three hours it had shocked him out of his skin seeing her sitting there in one piece and not the victim of some noisy accident. His concern turned to anger.

She didn't answer him, just looked from him to the screen where a programme still played. He followed the direction of her stare, his frown deepening as he recognised the rerun of the programme that had outraged his sister so much a few months earlier.

Swearing softly, he walked across to the wall and pulled out the plug.

After the deafening noise the smothering silence was profound. Anna could hear her own heartbeat.

'What are you watching that rubbish for?' His deep accusing voice sounded loud in the sudden silence. He extended his hand, impatiently flicking the cuff of his shirt so that he could read the time on the face of the silver wristwatch. 'It's half one in the morning. Why aren't you asleep?'

'Why aren't you?' She laughed. How typical of Cesare to blame her for something that was not her fault.

'What is funny?' He had spent the last three hours fighting the impulse to walk through that door. Now he had and the question was, would he be able to walk back out? Did he even want to?

Stupid question, of course he didn't want to, but a man could not always have what he wanted even when it was within grabbing distance. Soft, warm and sweet-smelling and within... His jaw clenched down hard as he bit out a savage epithet.

His anger rolled over her, but she didn't mind. It was proof that he was alive, that she was alive. A fact that should, she realised, be celebrated, not taken for granted. Cesare was standing there and he very nearly had not been. A miracle, they'd called it, and they were right. It was a miracle. Life was so fragile. Anna had never realised just how fragile until that moment.

It had taken seeing him almost die, a glimpse of a world that did not contain arrogant, unreasonable, breathtakingly beautiful Cesare Urquart, for her to realise that she wasn't just in lust with him. Somehow she had fallen in love.

'Did you hear me? It's half past one in the morning.' Conscious he was repeating himself, he lowered his gaze and found his attention drawn to the silky curve of smooth skin, exposed where the baggy neckline of the skimpy nightshirt she wore had slipped over her shoulder. He was unable to halt his hungry scrutiny and it travelled down, lingering on the length of slim, shapely leg. In his head he saw himself sliding his hand beneath the hem to cup her smooth, rounded bottom before tugging the shirt over her head to reveal those soft, sinuous curves.

Grinding his teeth, he swallowed and dragged his eyes back to her face. No make-up, hair a burnished messy tangle and faint purplish shadows under her bluer than blue eyes. It should have been a massive turn-off for a man who expected nothing less than perfect grooming from the women who shared his bed. Should be but wasn't. Somehow she managed to look more soul-destroyingly sexy than any woman he had ever seen.

Anna got to her feet still reeling from the emotive impact of her shocking self-discovery. She was horrified and delighted then, with a dramatic change of mood, hotly furious.

'Why would you want to do that?' Wasn't life dangerous enough without going out looking for ways to kill yourself...to the extent of choosing a career that involved risking your neck on a daily basis?

'Do what?' The nightshirt was short—very short. Distracted, he did not register her expression until she was close enough to touch him, and she did, but not in the way he had imagined. She threw a punch that landed in the centre of his chest. For a tiny thing she was strong.

'What the…? He caught her wrists before she could repeat the performance.

Her eyes wild, she struggled for about ten seconds before she collapsed without warning against his chest and gave one dry, pain-filled sob that felt like a knife sinking into his chest.

Cesare wondered if he might have had a clue what was going on if he hadn't been struggling to control his baser instincts. As it was he didn't. He didn't know what to do. He had known what to do since he was fourteen and since that moment had rarely experienced a second of indecision. As he looked down at the top of her flame-bright head pressed into his chest, Cesare heard himself blurt, 'I didn't mean to yell.'

She lifted her head and stepped backwards, conscious of a feeling of deprivation as she lost contact with his hard warmth. 'I suppose you didn't mean to nearly kill yourself either?' Her swimming azure eyes slid of their own volition to the blank television screen; a deep shudder stole through her body and she looked away quickly.

'Oh, that.' He tore his thoughts away from sex and focused on an argument he had polished over the years. This was not the first time he had been called upon to defend his choice of profession, though possibly the first time anyone had made their argument quite so physically. 'Statistically speaking these days Formula One is actually extremely safe. Now if you want to talk danger horse-racing is—'

Statistics! Anna didn't believe what she was hearing. She had made the most monumental discovery in her life and he was standing there looking drop-dead gorgeous talking about statistics and horses?

'The fact is I could get killed crossing the road tomorrow.'

If he carried on talking that way he wouldn't have to wait that long, she thought grimly. She could see a dozen gaping holes in his spurious argument she could have challenged him on, but she made her point with a sarcastic, 'That's a very original argument.'

His lips twitched.

'I'm sorry if I was over the top but I've not been sleeping that well.' Then, aware that sleep deprivation hardly satisfactorily explained her outburst, she tacked on reluctantly, 'I was in a car crash when I was a kid.'

'You have nightmares?' The doctors had warned him that this might happen for him but it never had. He had put his escape down to a lack of imagination, although his imagination was putting in some overtime at the moment!

Anna shook her head. 'No, I don't remember it, but my parents were killed and I suppose the idea of someone deliberately—' She managed a shrug. 'I guess it just hit a nerve seeing that. But that's your choice. I had no right to go for you like that.'

'I'm sorry about your parents.'

He sounded sincere, not just like someone trotting out a response. Anna met his eyes and saw he was. She felt desire drift through her and looked away quickly before she walked across to one of the sofas and sank down. 'You lost your parents too.'

He came, not to sit down, but to stand behind the sofa opposite, his big hands on the brocade back. He had beautiful hands like the rest of him, strong and capable; his tapering fingers were sensitive and long. She felt a stab of sheer longing as she thought about how they would feel on her skin. 'My mother is still alive.'

Her gaze lifted. 'Oh, yes, you said. I forgot. Does she live in Italy?' Presumably he had family there? Anna had a mental vision of a big warm family with lots of babies…Cesare's babies would be beautiful.

'My mother does not live any place for long.' He gave a quick smile but his voice was hard as he added, 'She has a very low boredom threshold.'

Anna recalled Angel using those exact same words. 'You must have missed your father after the divorce.'

The housekeeper normally guarded the family secrets as if they were the crown jewels, but in a rare garrulous moment Mrs Mack had unbent enough to reveal that Cesare had been nine when his parents had split up.

'My mother was granted custody but Dad got us in the holidays.'

'It must be hard for a woman to be apart from her children.'

'My mother never had much time for her children.'

It was the casual way he said it that shocked Anna almost more than what he said.

'She only took us because she knew our father wanted us. Our wishes never even crossed her mind. When we were younger she treated us like fashion accessories and when we were older and less cute we were more encumbrances. But, unlike Angel, I was not competition.' He stopped abruptly and Anna saw shock move across his lean face.

He read the sympathy glowing in her expressive eyes and visibly winced. He did not invite sympathy; he was allergic to it.

Anna could almost hear the sound of the shutters falling in place.

'So I will leave you to get some sleep.' It was a plan, definitely a plan, but somehow his feet stayed where they were.

'I'm awake. You were right, you know, you do never know when it's going to happen. I could walk under a bus tomorrow.'

'I think it unlikely.' There was a glitter in her eyes that he had never seen before. He found it mesmerising.

'But it could happen. Perhaps it is a good idea to treat every day as though it's your last?'

'I didn't say that, and you are not going to die tomorrow.'

'But if I did,' she mused, looking up at him through her lashes, 'I'd be a virgin.' She took a deep breath and lifted her chin, delivering a direct look. 'I don't want to die a virgin, Cesare.'

'I think that unlikely,' he rasped thickly. The seconds ticked by and Cesare could feel his control trickling away, like water down a drain.

'Anna,' he warned as she got up from the sofa. 'Just stay over there, don't...' She didn't stop, she just carried on coming until she was standing right there beside him. 'This is a very bad idea. I'm not the sort of man—'

'I know what sort of man you are, Cesare,' she cut in, thinking how weirdly calm she sounded. Inside she was anything but. Inside she could not believe she was saying these things; she could not believe the person she was saying them to.

He was the exact opposite of everything she found attractive in a man. She didn't even like him yet she had fallen in love with him.

'I'm a virgin, not stupid. Relax, I'm not asking you to marry me. I don't want your mind or... Just have sex with me.' She caught her plump lower lip between her teeth and husked, 'If you want to?'

The throaty whisper, the sultry pout... Want? Considering the need that was pounding through his body, under other circumstances he might have laughed, but he couldn't even manage an ironic smile. His facial muscles were locked tight. It was taking every last ounce of his will power not to deliver what she was begging him for. This might be many men's secret fantasy but not his. The reminder did not reach his raging arousal.

'It's not a question of want, Anna.' But he did want her with an intensity that he had not felt in a long time, if ever. He struggled to think past the relentless raging need to touch, taste, possess.

Anna shook her head, her eyelashes fluttering against her warm cheeks as she swallowed the hurt, hearing only irritation in his harsh response. 'Fine, forget I said it.'

Later he told himself that it was the shadow of uncertainty he saw deep in her violet-blue eyes, the realisation that her confident act was not even skin deep, that broke him.

He allowed himself a mental image of them together in bed. He met the blue eyes lifted to his and, no longer thinking, just acting—*Dio*, but it was a relief to let the constraints go— he stepped towards her, bringing up one hand to rest on the indent of her waist as he brushed the knuckles of his free hand along her cheek. He felt her gasp and tremble.

Anna watched his eyes darken with predatory intent and could hardly breathe, the excitement fizzing through her veins was so intense. She met him half-way as he pulled her into his body, letting her feel how much he wanted her.

'Are you sure about this?' If she said no he might have to spend the night in a cold shower.

Her lips almost brushed his skin as she reached up to whisper, 'Totally.'

Her body still stretched in an arc towards him, she linked her slim arms around his strong neck. He slid his hands down her narrow back until he reached her waist, then, splaying his fingers he cupped her deliciously firm bottom, pressing a kiss to the exposed curve of her neck before he lifted her until she was on eye level with him.

Her breath was coming in fast, shallow, excited bursts as she wrapped her lovely long legs around his hips to secure her position. The casual display of male strength—he had lifted her as if she weighed nothing—was quite incredibly arousing.

'Are you sure you've never done this before?' he slurred.

The blue of her eyes was almost entirely obscured by the dilated pupils as she stared at him with the intensity of someone committing each feature, each angle and line of his face to memory.

He stared back, feeling his blood heat as he gazed at the pouty, pink outline of her lips.

'I'm a bad case of arrested development.'

The barely leashed passion in his deep, drowning kiss made her moan, the sound lost in his mouth. Swept away by the dormant passion that stirred to life, she kissed him back, meeting his tongue with her own and feeling a dizzy rush as they connected. Deep in her belly, the ache intensified, the heat pooling in liquid warmth between her thighs, and her skin prickled with heat. She wanted him so much it hurt but a secret fear remained: the spectres of tall blonde goddesses still made her hold back.

'I hope you'll make some allowances, Cesare,' she whispered into his mouth. 'I'm not—'

The throaty whisper, the sultry, scared little smile obliterated the last shreds of rational thought. Still carrying her, he strode towards the door. 'You are a sexy, crazy little red-headed witch. I haven't known down from up since I saw you.'

'I am?'

His reply was a drowning kiss that snapped her head back.

'Can you taste how much I need you?'

If that was what need tasted like it might become her favourite food. 'Delicious. You taste delicious.' She squeezed her eyes tight closed as she punctuated each fervent word with a kiss pressed to his beautiful mouth.

It wasn't until she opened her eyes that she realised they were no longer in the sitting room or the bedroom. 'What, where...?' she cried as he kicked the door open.

'I've been seeing you in my bed since the moment I laid eyes on you.'

'I've been seeing you naked.'

Her bold admission was rewarded with a sizzling look from his darkened spiky-lashed eyes. 'Looks like this is the night we have our wishes come true, *cara*.'

He was her dream, Anna thought. She held tight as he carried her at breakneck speed up the same staircase she had taken very recently.

The door of his bedroom was already open. The room was lit by a single lamp that burned on a low table beside the window. The yellow light was supplanted by the moonlight that shone in through the mullioned windows.

Cesare took her directly to the big four-poster bed that dominated the massive but relatively sparsely furnished room. Anna had no eyes for the décor, just for the man who held her. Holding her eyes, he laid her on it, pushing a pile of cushions away with his hand as he came to kneel over her.

He stroked his fingers down her cheek, spread the shiny mass of curls around her face and very slowly bent his head and kissed her.

Her chest lifted with the fractured sigh that locked

in her chest. She moaned when he lifted his head. She was literally burning up with lust. She had never imagined feeling this much...wanting this much.

'This is why people who aren't crazy get pregnant.'

She wasn't aware of having voiced the discovery until he cupped her chin in his hand and said fiercely, 'I won't let that happen to you. Just relax. I'll look after things.'

It required no effort to do as he suggested because crazily she trusted implicitly the man she had spent every waking moment hating since they had met. Somewhere in all that hating she had fallen in love.

The words that she knew she couldn't speak were in her head. She grabbed his head, framing it between her hands and kissed him hard to stop herself. 'I know you will, but I need...don't stop touching me, Cesare,' she begged thickly. 'I really need...'

'Tell me,' he urged, watching his control leave the room. She was just too tempting, too gorgeous, too hot for him. His powerful chest lifted as her deep drowning blue eyes opened.

'I just need you.' She reached up and began to unfasten the buttons on his shirt, pulling the fabric back as she worked her way upwards to reveal the defined slabs of muscle on his washboard-flat belly and the hair-roughened triangle on his otherwise smooth chest. His skin was like silk. She spread her fingers and let them glide with gloating pleasure over the warm surface, revelling in her first experience of sexual female power as Cesare sucked in a painful breath and groaned.

She was reaching for the belt of his trousers when

he grabbed her hand, and, taking possession of her free hand planted them above her head.

He only stayed there suspended above her for a few moments but that was long enough for Anna to make a shattering discovery: surrender was a turn-on.

Trusting another person enough to surrender control was wildly exciting. Before she could properly explore the amazing possibilities of this discovery she found herself lying face to face, lips to lips, chest to chest, thigh to thigh with Cesare, whose long, lean, gorgeously hard length was lying beside her.

His heavy hand lay in the indent of her waist. The other sliding up under her nightshirt, along the smooth skin of her thigh and higher to her bottom, caused her to gasp.

She closed her eyes. His were burning too bright. The aching thickness in her throat made it impossible for her to articulate her feelings even had she known what they were, but it turned out it didn't matter. He knew, he knew where to touch and how. He touched her everywhere until she simply couldn't bear it any longer. It was then she realised that she was naked.

'You're perfect.'

Anna felt the tension drain from her shoulders. She was. She really was. She could be anything Cesare said, anything he wanted.

He couldn't take his eyes off her. Looking at her sleek and slender body was everything he imagined and more. Hardly able to breathe, he cupped one plump, perfect breast in his hand even though he knew it threatened his already shaky control. The simple act of tast-

ing the tight rosy bud, watching her face as he drew it
into his mouth, was more erotic, more arousing than
anything he could remember. For a long time sex had
been an exercise, something he could do well, the moves
planned and mapped. He was able to stand back, pre-
dict his partner's response, even congratulate himself
because he knew the beautifully choreographed coupling was visual perfection.

Satisfaction guaranteed every time, mocked the voice
in his head, because Cesare knew the moves and he got
ten out of ten for artistic interpretation, and so as a rule
did his partner. Smooth, slick and satisfying—so what
if he felt empty later? It looked good.

Anna was beautiful, but this was not about perfection, it was about raw, visceral feeling. He growled his
rampant, throaty appreciation before he lifted his head
and moved his thumb across the tight centre, drawing
a shocked gasp that became a hoarse groan as his lips
and tongue replaced the digit. This was no show-house
coupling. It was raw and urgent and gloriously messy.
Cesare had discovered chaos and he loved it!

Even in the midst of chaos he retained the knowledge that this was her first time, and it was his duty,
his privilege, to make this experience a good one for
her. But, God, she made it hard. How was a man meant
to hold back when those hands, that mouth, they were
everywhere?

As he stroked her stomach, his touch leaving hot
trails on her skin, Anna could hardly bear it. Then he
slid down her body and parted her thighs. The first

touch of his fingers between her thighs made her stiffen in shock.

Then it was all right because he was feeding her hand onto his body, letting her feel him and then a moment later unzipping his pants to give her access to his erection.

'Oh, yes…'

'Absolutely,' he agreed, kissing her as he slid his hand between her thighs. 'That's right,' he encouraged as she parted them for him.

The heat flooding her face prickled like a dark tide under her skin as he separated the protective folds and touched the tight nub, rubbing his finger across the sensitised flesh until she couldn't breathe, until she protested.

'I can't do this.'

'Oh, yes, you can, *cara*,' he promised, pulling away, but only to kick off his pants. Then, naked, he rejoined her. 'You're brilliant at this.'

Her awed glance slid down his long, lean body, trying not to linger too obviously on his arousal. He was breath-takingly perfect and obviously, even to her inexperienced eyes, very well endowed. 'I am?' Her fingers curled around his erection, drawing a deep groan. 'Oh yes, I am.'

When he slid a finger into her, a long, low, feral moan emerged from her parted lips. Desperate now, Anna reached for him. Cesare was breathing soft, soothing, sexy words into her ears. It didn't really matter she understood not a word of Italian, the hypnotic sound had a hypnotic effect.

The sense of eerie calm lasted as he slid into her. The pain much less than she had anticipated as her body stretched to accommodate him. Loving him hot and hard inside her, loving his weight pressing her down. Then, as he slid deeper into her slick, tight wetness, a switch flicked on in her brain. No longer calm, Anna was consumed by a frantic wild desperation to take all his hot velvet hardness into her.

'More!' she gritted, bucking beneath him, her nails digging into his shoulders, and he responded to her urging.

The end came so abruptly, so strongly that she saw black dots dance before her eyes as the pleasure of that final release drove her to the brink of consciousness. But she didn't fall, she flew, feeling his hot release as she reached the stars.

'Well, it's obvious why you were a virgin. Like the man said, you're frigid.'

Anna opened one eye and stretched languorously. 'I'm laughing inside.' Actually inside she was feeling muscles she hadn't known she had.

He stroked her body. 'So what's the story? There must have been men.'

Anna raised herself up on one elbow, feeling weirdly comfortable with their naked states and his interested stare...

'You never seen a naked woman before?'

'I've never seen a naked you before. Good God, Anna, what were the men in your life thinking of?' How was it possible for this innately sensual creature to be untouched? It was as if, like a fairy-tale princess, she had been asleep. Hell, he was no prince. 'You do know that this is just sex?'

'I mentioned that I had a romance. It wasn't all that it's cracked up to be—I was engaged.' The hand on her bottom stilled. 'The computer matched us. It was a celibate relationship, more a meeting of minds, but he respected me,' she mocked with a laugh. 'Though not, as it turned out, as much as he respected the underwear model he ran off with a week before the wedding.'

'What a loser!'

Anna rolled on her back, his automatic scorn healing the unacknowledged wounds the rejection had inflicted on her pride. 'I like to think so.'

'His loss, my gain.' Expression intent, he paused, his hand halfway to her plump breast. 'You do know that—'

'You want me for my body? No problem. I want you for yours.' The lie came easily. She'd have done anything, said anything, to have this last a bit longer.

CHAPTER ELEVEN

TWO WEEKS LATER the lie came a lot less easily.

Over that time the sex stayed incredible but Anna was tortured by the knowledge that, for him at least, it would burn itself out and she was constantly alert to the signs, preferring to jump before she was pushed.

That way she would be left with memories and a modicum of pride. The decision made her feel mature and in control.

In the end she wasn't prepared at all. Anna didn't see the end coming until it was thrown on her bed, shiny and sparkling in the guise of diamonds. Her reaction was neither mature or controlled.

'I miss you so much when you're not here. I wish…I really wish…love…'

As the sleepy words translated in his head ultra-controlled, fearless Cesare experienced a moment of sheer gut-wrenching alien panic, followed a second later by utter rejection.

He might not have even heard the sleepy confession or the wistful addition had he not been too exhausted to move her after a wild and lengthy session of love-mak-ing. He did now, disconnecting their damp bodies as he slid off her. The sex these past weeks had been noth-ing like anything he had ever experienced, but it was just sex. She knew that. Feeling his resentment rise, he looked at her sleeping face with a mingling of messy emotions. Anger, fascination, compulsion.

And, oblivious, she lay curled up, her head tucked into the angle of his shoulder. Part of him, the cowardly part, desperately wanted to ignore what he had heard. The seemingly innocent words were not the problem but the response they required was.

He did not miss her.

Missing required a need, and Cesare did not need anyone.

The night before had been incredible so when she woke to find him fully dressed and announcing that he would be in London for the rest of the week she didn't know how to respond.

Ruling out grabbing his leg and begging him not to go, she pulled the sheet up to her chin and struggled to sound okay with the idea of not seeing him for the next five days…and nights!

'I-I didn't realise.' She swept the tangle of curls from her face, glanced at the clock and saw it was still only five in the morning. 'I'll make you coffee.'

He shook his head, the stammer always melted him. 'No, I'm fine.'

A furrow pleated her brow. He didn't look fine or

sound fine. Distant was the word that came to mind when she looked at him.

'Angel is back on Tuesday?'

She nodded.

'I don't know if you've discussed it, so when you leave is obviously between you two.' He saw the look of shock on her face, the hurt reflected in her blue eyes and told himself this was the right thing to do, easier in the long run.

He couldn't give her what she wanted.

'But if I don't see you...'

Another man would give her what she wanted.

Cesare closed his eyes and breathed through a blast of white-hot jealous fury and reached into his pocket as he cleared his throat.

'If I don't see you before...'

Her brow furrowed. Anna didn't immediately realise what it was he had casually tossed onto the bed, then as she picked it up and recognised what it was her expression froze. The warmth drained from her body; she was ice.

'What is this?' she asked, no discernible expression in her flat voice as she stared at the sparkling diamond bracelet she held between her fingers.

'You don't like it?' He shrugged. 'No problem—you can return it and exchange it for something more to your taste if you prefer.'

No problem? No problem being treated like some sort of call girl paid for services rendered? Her chest tight with the emotions clenched like a fist there, Anna exhaled a long, slow, shaky breath and in one motion swept back the sheet and got to her feet. She was naked, every pale inch of her shivering with fury.

She tossed back her hair and took a step towards him, arching a haughty brow as she pinned him with a frosty, iridescent blue stare.

Unable to retain eye contact, Cesare looked downwards, his darkened eyes greedily caressing every inch of her pearly, sleek, quivering body. She was the living, breathing embodiment of his darkest fantasies.

'And if I prefer the money?' she challenged, baring her white teeth in a parody of a smile.

The comment enabled Cesare to drag his rampant stare back to her face. His dark brows flattened into a disapproving straight line as he rasped, 'Do not be stupid.'

'Why stupid?' she asked, affecting elaborate surprise. 'Isn't this a payment for services rendered?' Her lips twisted with distaste as she stared at the bracelet.

He swore and wondered if one day he might be able to appreciate the irony—the one time in his life he had ever felt compelled to walk into a jeweller's because something in the window had made him think of her.

'Do not act like a call girl. This is not you.' He clenched his teeth and struggled for a level of calm. 'If you do not like it—'

'And if you don't like me acting like a call girl don't treat me like one!' she yelled, flinging the bracelet at him.

Without taking his eyes from her face, he reached out and caught the glittering projectile.

'Like it!' she all but screamed. 'I hate it and I hate you. How dare you insult me with your crappy bracelets? If you're bored just say so, that's fine, but don't you dare try and pay me off!'

His jaw clenched, Cesare let the bracelet fall to the floor from his lax fingers and dragged a hand through his dark hair.

This was not going well.

And you really expected this to end well, Cesare? asked the wry voice in his head.

She was being unreasonable, shrill, emotional. She was being all the things he hated and he wanted to hold her, he wanted to take her in his arms and lay her on the bed...

She was being Anna.

'I cannot do this.'

Anna blinked back the tears filling her eyes. 'Oh, yes, you can. You've had a lot of practice. This is a first for me.'

Did she think he needed reminding?

She swallowed past the restriction in her throat. 'So, sorry if I'm behaving like a human bloody being.' With a sob she flung herself on the bed face down.

Anna thought she felt his hand on her hair, but she must have imagined it because later when she rolled over the room was empty and her eyes were red and puffy.

Anna, her eyes still puffy and swollen from the crying jag, pushed away the memory of the monumental fight—she supposed the moment your heart broke was bound to linger—and struggled to focus on what Angel was saying.

'So what time is your flight tomorrow?' Tomorrow she would be effectively surplus to requirements and it looked as though Cesare had already moved on, which was no shock. It might have been what she had anticipated, but he could have waited until she had packed her bags; he might have waited around to say goodbye.

'Actually I…is Cesare around?'

Anna shook her head, and then, remembering that Angel couldn't see her, dropped the fake smile and said, 'No.' She watched him on the screen, stalking down the red carpet and distracting the bubbly female presenter from her designated Hollywood targets and using the minor royal on his arm as an excuse to shove a microphone in his face and touch his arm…repeatedly.

Cesare, looking dark and enigmatic, produced a curt monosyllabic response to the woman's gushing questions but this did not seem to throw her at all.

'That's something.'

'I don't suppose…do you have your passport with you?'

'I think so,' Anna confirmed dully. The minor royal, looking visibly amused, seemed content to stand back and watch as the interviewer became increasingly flirtatious. And why not? She could afford to smile; she knew that behind closed doors he was all hers.

Jealousy, Anna discovered, was not just a state of mind. It involved physical pain.

'That's great.' The relief in Angel's voice was tangible. 'I have the most enormous favour to ask.'

Anna half listened, growing more attentive when Cesare and his partner walked into the theatre and escaped the media scrutiny. Angel got Anna's full attention when she realised the favour involved her getting on a plane and putting several hundred air miles between her and Cesare. She was more than happy to agree to Angel's plan and, Angel being Angel, she had everything organised down to the last detail.

Anna was so happy it didn't even cross her mind to ask why Angel's plans had changed.

'Your tickets will be at the airport and probably best not to give Jas anything heavy to eat as she's not the greatest traveller in the world. I'll meet you at the airport and take you back to the hotel. I've booked you into one of the garden bungalows for a week.'

'That's lovely of you, but actually I can't stay so this trip—it's just the airport for me. I'll deliver Jas to you and then have to fly straight back to the UK. I've got an interview on Thursday.' She had intended to tell Cesare that today, and secretly she had hoped he would— what? Beg her not to go? Suggest they stay in touch? Look mildly unhappy? God, how had she let this happen? How had she been so stupid?

'Oh, no, why didn't you say? Forget I asked. I'll sort something else. I had hoped not to get Cesare involved but—no problem. So tell me about the job.'

'The school has an excellent reputation,' Anna said, trying to inject the enthusiasm she knew she should be feeling into her voice. 'But there's no reason I can't bring Jas out. I want to help, really.'

'You can't fly out here, turn around and fly back.

Definitely not,' Angel protested. 'I couldn't ask you to do that.'

'You're not asking. I'm offering to chaperone Jasmine.'

'It would be good to keep Cesare out of this until it's sorted,' Angel admitted. 'Obviously I'll let him know once Jas is here.'

'Obviously.' Actually there was nothing obvious about any of this to Anna.

'It's just Cesare…he can be a bit overprotective.'

Not of me, Anna thought bitterly.

'You really wouldn't mind?'

'Not at all.'

'You're a star,' Angel enthused. 'And you haven't even asked why I want you to bring Jas out here. I was going to say don't ask, but it's not a secret, or it won't be soon. The fact is, I want Jas to meet her father.'

'Wow!'

A nervous laugh came down the line and a breathless, 'Pretty wow, but don't say anything to Jas.'

'Of course not.'

'Or, of course, Cesare.'

'Don't worry.'

Leaking patience from every pore by the time he had made a rapid tour of the castle and immediate grounds, Cesare was in a dangerous mood. He had left the glittering party midway through, abandoned his beautiful partner, probably offending one of his best friends in the process. He rather doubted he would still be best man at their wedding that summer. He'd driven up from London.

Had he been a man in a desert seeking life-sustaining water the urgency that held him in its grip during that journey could not have been greater.

Cesare stared at his housekeeper in disbelief. 'What do you mean gone? Where has she gone to?'

'To the airport with Ja—'

'Airport!' Cesare launched his stinging attack before the woman had time to deliver her explanation. Stabbing his fingers into his hair in a gesture of extreme frustration, he began to pace the floor like a caged panther.

He paused and flung the woman another scathing look. 'You let her go to the airport?'

'It was hardly my place to stop her.'

He stopped pacing and thought, No, it was mine.

And had he been able or willing to say what she wanted to hear, say what he had been too stubborn to admit he wanted to, he would have been here to prevent her running away.

All she had said was—'*I miss you so much when you're not here.*' And he had panicked.

He made a conscious effort to slow his breathing, recognising this situation was one of his own making. This was the result of his inability to accept that in a few short weeks she had become a part of his life. As he had searched for Anna, his home, the place he felt an almost physical connection with and which, like his ancestors, he would have done anything to preserve, had felt like a series of empty rooms. The reason had not hit him until Mrs Mack had delivered her killing blow—Anna was not in them—and it wasn't just the house her absence affected. *He* was empty without her.

But of course he would bring her back.

He had sent her away with his talk of just sex. She had given him herself totally, held nothing back and he had said it was just sex. He had seen he was killing her with his coldness and then he had crowned the insult with the damned bracelet, which she had thrown back in his face. The muscles in his face relaxed enough to allow the corners of his mouth to lift as he recalled her fiery reaction.

Anna was the least avaricious person he had ever met. He loved that about her. Had he ever really thought she would do anything but throw it at him? Had he unconsciously been trying to push her away, make her reject him?

He'd been trying to put barriers between them from the moment they met, and why? Because he knew she was different, he knew she was not someone he could eject from his bed in the middle of the night, not someone he could walk away from. She made him feel everything he had never wanted to feel, everything he thought would make him weak.

Cesare's mouth twisted in a sneer of self-disgust before he took a deep calming breath and tipped his head, offering a stiff smile of apology to his housekeeper. 'Where was she flying to?'

'Miss Angel arranged that side of things. I believe she is meeting them at the airport.'

He had not been expecting that! 'Angel?' When had his little sister got involved? 'Anna doesn't even like sunbathing!' he yelled, thinking of her lying on a white-sanded tropical beach being lusted after by a bunch of lecherous creeps who were fascinated by her creamy skin.

He closed his eyes and swore at length, only remembering his audience when he opened them again and saw the tight-lipped disapproval on the face of the woman who had known him since he was a boy.

'I'm quite sure that Miss Henderson will use sun block. She is extremely capable.'

Cesare was already pulling out his mobile phone and punching in numbers.

Anna felt her throat tighten as Jas, her nose pressed to the window of the Jeep her mother drove, waved goodbye. She stayed where she was until the Jeep vanished, then, blinking away emotional tears, walked back towards the terminal building and its air conditioning.

The heat had hit her the moment she stepped onto the tarmac. It had felt like walking into a solid wall. Jas, on the other hand, had revived the moment she disembarked. In seconds she had gone from looking like a wan little ghost to literally bouncing good health.

Anna envied her her youthful powers of recovery. She felt a hundred! When Angel had said Jas was not a good traveller, in her naivety Anna had felt quite confident about coping with a nauseous and possibly fretful child. How wrong had she been!

It had broken her heart to see the little girl so distressed and the journey had taken on a nightmare quality, not least because of the dirty looks they had received

from a certain section of passengers. Now, after standing out in the sun for a few minutes, she felt like a wilted
flower. Given time she might acclimatise to this sort of
environment, but Anna knew she would never acquire
a golden glowing tan like Angel.

Besides she liked the variety of living somewhere
where you could experience every weather known to
man in the space of twenty-four hours. Her smile faded
as it hit her, the finality of it. She wasn't going back to
Scotland. Her return ticket was for the far more tem-
perate capital.

Absently, she thought of home. She had spent a long
time getting her flat just as she wanted, decorating it
on a shoestring and furnishing it with recycled quirky
items that she had personalised. Being back home
should have felt like a good thing, but it didn't. Loving Cesare had changed so much. A place no longer
made her feel centred and at home, but a person—the
wrong person.

Would anywhere ever feel like home again? Even if
it meant she carried this awful black stone around in
her chest for the rest of her life she would never regret
loving him. The sad acknowledgement was tinged with
defiance, which enabled her to close off her feelings
behind a brittle shell.

Inside the terminal building she wandered towards
the duty-free outlets. Not because she felt the need of
retail therapy, but because she had a three-hour wait
before her return flight boarded and she was already
awash with coffee.

She spotted an outlet that sold handmade baby

clothes in brightly coloured ethnic prints. Knowing that the quirky items would appeal to Rosie, she'd actually spent half an hour selecting some of the cute but overpriced sleepsuits in several sizes after she realised how quickly babies grew.

Paying for her purchases, she walked out of the door and straight into a tall man who was striding past. She might have fallen if hands had not shot out to steady her.

Pre-programmed to apologise, she stuttered a shaken, 'S-sorry.' Then felt a stab of exasperation. The great oaf was the one at fault; he was the one who hadn't been looking where he was going.

'It's going to take a lot more than a sorry.'

The grim comment shattered her protective shell into a million pieces. 'Cesare, what are you...?' Blinking up at the tall figure towering over her, she shook her head, seriously considering the possibility that she had lost her mind.

'We need to talk.'

Her initial hastily formed impression had been that he was furious, but now Anna realised this was not the case. Emotions of a strong nature were rolling off him, but it was not anger that was causing the corded muscles of his neck to stand out, or that pulled the muscles of his face taut. Like an addict coming face to face with the drug of her choice, she couldn't stop shaking, or looking.

She cleared her throat. 'She's not here,' Anna prefaced and received a blank look. 'Angel has already picked her up.'

His dark brows knitted into a frown over his slate-grey eyes. 'Jas is here?'

'I assumed...' She shook her head and thought, Never a good idea with Cesare. 'I don't understand.' Leaving aside the why, there was a massive how? 'You were in London. I saw you on the television. The princess is very beautiful.' She bit her quivering lower lip.

'Olivia, a nice woman but boring. All she did was witter on endlessly about Rafe.'

'Who is Rafe?'

'The man she is going to marry.' He studied her face, then grinned. 'You were jealous.' He seemed to take a lot of pleasure from the discovery.

She set her mouth. Had there been a cat in hell's chance of her carrying it off she'd have lied. As there wasn't she simply toughed it out. 'I'll get over it,' she promised grimly.

His smile suddenly died. 'Well, I won't. If I saw you with another man I'd...'

This dog-in-the-manger attitude ignited the smouldering embers of Anna's resentment. Talk about mixed messages! He was the one who sent her away and now he was here saying stuff that had her fighting the urge to announce there was no other man for her and there never would be.

'Well, what do you expect me to do?' she asked him, struggling to maintain her uncaring façade. 'Take a vow of celibacy because you don't want me but you don't want anyone else to have me either?'

'I do want you,' he gritted. 'I need you, Anna.'

Wanting was good, needing was even better. The look of desperation etched on his lean face appeared genuine, but she couldn't lay herself open to that hurt, not again.

She was worn down by fatigue and unhappiness and the mask slipped as she raised her swimming blue eyes to him. 'You didn't want me there when you came back,' she wailed, unable to hold back the tears any longer. They spilled unchecked down her cheeks. It had been a total shock. She had always known that at some point the novelty of having her in his bed would pall, but the rejection had come totally out of the blue and hurt all the more because of it.

'I can't tell you how many times I almost turned the car around and came back, but I was just too gutless to admit I wanted to even to myself.'

'So why are you here, Cesare?'

He loosed a hoarse laugh. 'Why the hell do you think I'm here? I arrived back at Killaran to find you had run away.' With eyes that shone like the beaten silver bracelet she wore he pinned her with a fierce, hungry, soul-searing stare.

'I came to bring you back.'

Aware that her interpretation was coloured by her deep longing, against all her screaming instincts she adopted a breathless 'wait and see' policy and didn't react to this raw pronouncement. It did not mean that she had any control over the surge of tingling heat that washed over her skin, or the butterflies that were rioting in her stomach.

The man had followed her—that had to mean something, right?

Cesare clenched his teeth in frustration when his

words had no visible effect on her. He refused to acknowledge the doom-laden voice in his head that was telling him he'd blown it. Instead he took her wrist and pulled it against his chest. 'Come home with me.'

'This isn't the way home,' she gasped as she struggled to keep up with him while he virtually dragged her out through the revolving glass doors of the terminal building.

'This is the way to the company jet. How did you think I got here, *cara*?' he asked in response to her wide-eyed stare. 'We cannot have a conversation in that glass bowl.'

Anna squeezed her eyes half closed to cut down on the glare. She rubbed her skin where his fingers had cut into the flesh. A spasm of pain crossed his features as he watched her.

'I hurt you.' With pain in his eyes he lifted her hand and pressed her wrist to his lips.

Anna pulled her hand back, but not before that light contact had sent a surge like lightning along her receptive nerve endings.

'You come out fighting. I sometimes forget what a delicate little thing you are.' This time she followed of her own volition, lengthening her stride to stay by his side as he walked towards the shade of a palm tree. Even under it the heat rising from the paved area beneath her feet was stifling. 'I came here to bring you home and I am not leaving without you. If making that happen means I have to crawl and grovel, I will.'

The solemn declaration brought tears to her eyes. 'I don't want you to crawl or grovel, Cesare. I just want you to…' She shook her head, aware that she wanted the impossible. Cesare might have discovered he still wanted her in his bed and once that would have been enough, but not now. She shouldn't settle; she deserved more.

'Love you?' he supplied gently when her voice faded.

She nodded, looking at him through her tears. 'I thought sex would be enough but it isn't. I want more.'

'So do I.' He expelled a long gusty sigh. With the sense of release came a bemusement. It was easy to say. Why had he made it such a massive thing?

Anna's mouth opened and stayed that way until he nudged her jaw closed with his thumb. 'The past leaves its mark on us all.' He raised an interrogative brow, inviting her comment.

Anna nodded.

'I have always had a warped view of relationships,' he admitted, with a frankness he would have struggled with in the not so distant past. 'My parents' marriage was a disaster. I despised my father for loving my mother even after she left him. Love destroyed him and in my mind I equated love with weakness, and my mother…!' His shoulders lifted in an expressive shrug as he vented a hard laugh. 'What can you say about her, except all that glitters is not gold? I think she has something missing. Do you know what I mean?' He angled an enquiring look down at her.

'I think so.' Her heart bursting with empathic tenderness she was wary of expressing, Anna reached a tentative hand to touch his arm, half expecting him to shrug her off. Her throat tightened when he smiled down at her.

'She never fails to disappoint. She lacks a conscience and even a basic sense of morality. Combined with her charm and an utterly hedonistic, selfish outlook on life, she leaves a trail of disaster in her wake.'

'I think you're allowed a few trust issues.'

The comment drew a laugh from Cesare.

'I trust you with my life, Anna.'

Anna went totally still.

'The question is do you trust me?'

Anna looked at the hand he held out to her and without hesitation put her own hand in it.

Cesare smiled and dug his free hand into his pocket. Anna glimpsed red velvet and shook her head. 'I don't want the bracelet.'

'This is not a bracelet.'

It was a ring, a beautiful circle of diamonds surrounding a fabulous sapphire. Anna stared at it in awe. 'Is this what I think it is?'

'If you think it's a commitment to spend our lives together then, yes, you're right.' He took her hand and slid the ring on her finger. 'This is a proposal. Anna, marry me? I'm an idiot but I love you.'

Anna stood frozen for a moment before she slowly lifted her glowing eyes to the tall man beside her. 'My idiot. Yes, please.'

With a wild whoop he swept her off her feet. 'Thank God. For a moment there I really thought I'd blown it...'

EPILOGUE

As THE SUN slowly sank below the horizon and the pink tinge faded from the ocean Anna lifted her gaze to the sails flapping overhead in the strong breeze that had sprung up after dinner.

'This is perfect,' she sighed, leaning back into the strong, hard body of her husband. His arms came around her and she rubbed her cheek against the hard muscle of his upper arm.

'How did you know?' Anna couldn't recall having confided her lifelong fascination for tall ships to Cesare.

She had dreamed of one day taking a cruise on one of those supremely elegant vessels, but never in her wildest dreams had she imagined owning one.

Teacher's Pet, a three-masted schooner complete with crew, had been her astonishing wedding present. Cesare claimed it was a 'buy one get one free' deal—a wedding gift and honeymoon in one. There hadn't been time for a honeymoon after the wedding, just a weekend in Paris where it rained every day but the newlyweds didn't notice. One day, Cesare promised, he'd show her the sights of Paris, a city he knew well, and not just the inside of their hotel-suite bedroom!

They had arrived back at Killaran on the Sunday, and Monday morning Anna had started her new job. She was now the new head of Killaran primary school.

Cesare had passed on the offer from the school governors when the woman who had been given the job originally had pulled out at the last minute. He had been wary of her reaction, assuring her that there had been no coercion on his part and she was nobody's second best.

Anna hadn't been able to resist winding him up just a little, but she had quickly put his mind at rest, assuring him that she didn't care if she got the job by default. Naturally she admitted with mock solemnity that it was a bit disappointing to discover that she was expected to work, even though she was marrying a wealthy man.

Her tongue-in-cheek teasing had drawn a retributional response, though as that retribution involved ending up in bed Anna didn't mind at all. Actually Cesare had been tremendously supportive of her decision and could be heard frequently boasting of his headmistress wife and her general brilliance.

'Steady,' Cesare said, chaining her to his side with strong arms as the ship lurched a little, causing her feet to slip on the wooden deck. Having dressed for dinner tonight, she was wearing a pair of impractical heels that matched the silk slip dress she had picked for this special occasion. Cesare didn't know yet how important. She felt a flurry of anxiety that twanged her sensitive stomach muscles as she wondered what his response would be.

'I thought you were the woman who dreamed of life

on the ocean waves?' he teased, glad of the excuse to hold her tight. 'You haven't even got your sea legs yet.'

Anna squirmed around in his arms to face him. 'I have!' she protested indignantly.

He arched a brow. 'It's no good pretending. I've heard you throwing up just this morning and yesterday—' He stopped dead as he took her face between his hands and levelled a long, searching look deep into her blue eyes. Whatever he saw there caused the blood to drain from his face. 'That wasn't sea sickness, was it?'

She shook her head and looked away, suddenly afraid to look in his eyes, afraid of what she might see there. They had discussed having a family before they were married and had both agreed it was something they both wanted...somewhere down the line.

How would he react to the news of the unplanned pregnancy? Anna didn't realistically expect him to be as ecstatically happy about the news as she was, but she didn't think she could bear it if he hated the idea. If he pretended to be all right with it.

'You're having our baby?'

Anna had not heard that note in his voice before, but it wasn't anger or disappointment.

'When...how...are you feeling? What did the doctor say...?'

The questions came thick, fast and eager until she pressed a finger to his lips, laughing. 'Slow down. I've only just found out myself.'

'You have not seen a doctor?'

She shook her head and admitted quietly, 'I thought it might be nice if we went together the first time.'

The stern disapproval melted from his face. 'Of course, but not the first time—every time. I will be with you every step of the way,' he promised, trying hard not to think about the birth. 'Come, sit down,' he urged, trailing a supportive arm around her shoulders. 'You should not be standing, and take off those shoes. They are lethal and if you fell—'

'So you are happy about this?'

He flashed her an incredulous look as he pressed her down into a chair and fell into a graceful squatting pose beside her. 'Are you joking? A baby! It's incredible.'

'Even if it wasn't planned?'

'Life is not about plans, *cara,* it is about love and hope and, now, babies. I'll get them to turn this damned thing around if anything were to happen while we were out in the middle of the ocean—'

'Nothing bad is going to happen, Cesare,' she soothed, grabbing his hands. She was able to speak with utter and total confidence as she added quietly, 'Not while I have you.'

'You will have me always, *cara*, for better or worse. I love you with all my heart…my soul…no, you are my soul. I believe that.'

Anna smiled, her heart in her eyes as she looked into the face of the beautiful man she loved.

'You said that once before, in front of witnesses. I believed you then and I always will,' she said simply.

* * * * *

Mills & Boon® Hardback

September 2013

ROMANCE

Challenging Dante	Lynne Graham
Captivated by Her Innocence	Kim Lawrence
Lost to the Desert Warrior	Sarah Morgan
His Unexpected Legacy	Chantelle Shaw
Never Say No to a Caffarelli	Melanie Milburne
His Ring Is Not Enough	Maisey Yates
A Reputation to Uphold	Victoria Parker
A Whisper of Disgrace	Sharon Kendrick
If You Can't Stand the Heat...	Joss Wood
Maid of Dishonour	Heidi Rice
Bound by a Baby	Kate Hardy
In the Line of Duty	Ami Weaver
Patchwork Family in the Outback	Soraya Lane
Stranded with the Tycoon	Sophie Pembroke
The Rebound Guy	Fiona Harper
Greek for Beginners	Jackie Braun
A Child to Heal Their Hearts	Dianne Drake
Sheltered by Her Top-Notch Boss	Joanna Neil

MEDICAL

The Wife He Never Forgot	Anne Fraser
The Lone Wolf's Craving	Tina Beckett
Re-awakening His Shy Nurse	Annie Claydon
Safe in His Hands	Amy Ruttan

Mills & Boon® Large Print

September 2013

ROMANCE

A Rich Man's Whim	Lynne Graham
A Price Worth Paying?	Trish Morey
A Touch of Notoriety	Carole Mortimer
The Secret Casella Baby	Cathy Williams
Maid for Montero	Kim Lawrence
Captive in his Castle	Chantelle Shaw
Heir to a Dark Inheritance	Maisey Yates
Anything but Vanilla...	Liz Fielding
A Father for Her Triplets	Susan Meier
Second Chance with the Rebel	Cara Colter
First Comes Baby...	Michelle Douglas

HISTORICAL

The Greatest of Sins	Christine Merrill
Tarnished Amongst the Ton	Louise Allen
The Beauty Within	Marguerite Kaye
The Devil Claims a Wife	Helen Dickson
The Scarred Earl	Elizabeth Beacon

MEDICAL

NYC Angels: Redeeming The Playboy	Carol Marinelli
NYC Angels: Heiress's Baby Scandal	Janice Lynn
St Piran's: The Wedding!	Alison Roberts
Sydney Harbour Hospital: Evie's Bombshell	Amy Andrews
The Prince Who Charmed Her	Fiona McArthur
His Hidden American Beauty	Connie Cox

Mills & Boon® Hardback
October 2013

ROMANCE

The Greek's Marriage Bargain	Sharon Kendrick
An Enticing Debt to Pay	Annie West
The Playboy of Puerto Banús	Carol Marinelli
Marriage Made of Secrets	Maya Blake
Never Underestimate a Caffarelli	Melanie Milburne
The Divorce Party	Jennifer Hayward
A Hint of Scandal	Tara Pammi
A Façade to Shatter	Lynn Raye Harris
Whose Bed Is It Anyway?	Natalie Anderson
Last Groom Standing	Kimberly Lang
Single Dad's Christmas Miracle	Susan Meier
Snowbound with the Soldier	Jennifer Faye
The Redemption of Rico D'Angelo	Michelle Douglas
The Christmas Baby Surprise	Shirley Jump
Backstage with Her Ex	Louisa George
Blame It on the Champagne	Nina Harrington
Christmas Magic in Heatherdale	Abigail Gordon
The Motherhood Mix-Up	Jennifer Taylor

MEDICAL

Gold Coast Angels: A Doctor's Redemption	Marion Lennox
Gold Coast Angels: Two Tiny Heartbeats	Fiona McArthur
The Secret Between Them	Lucy Clark
Craving Her Rough Diamond Doc	Amalie Berlin

Mills & Boon® Large Print
October 2013

ROMANCE

The Sheikh's Prize	Lynne Graham
Forgiven but not Forgotten?	Abby Green
His Final Bargain	Melanie Milburne
A Throne for the Taking	Kate Walker
Diamond in the Desert	Susan Stephens
A Greek Escape	Elizabeth Power
Princess in the Iron Mask	Victoria Parker
The Man Behind the Pinstripes	Melissa McClone
Falling for the Rebel Falcon	Lucy Gordon
Too Close for Comfort	Heidi Rice
The First Crush Is the Deepest	Nina Harrington

HISTORICAL

Reforming the Viscount	Annie Burrows
A Reputation for Notoriety	Diane Gaston
The Substitute Countess	Lyn Stone
The Sword Dancer	Jeannie Lin
His Lady of Castlemora	Joanna Fulford

MEDICAL

NYC Angels: Unmasking Dr Serious	Laura Iding
NYC Angels: The Wallflower's Secret	Susan Carlisle
Cinderella of Harley Street	Anne Fraser
You, Me and a Family	Sue MacKay
Their Most Forbidden Fling	Melanie Milburne
The Last Doctor She Should Ever Date	Louisa George

0913 GEN STD LP